STARS
IN YOUR EYES

STARS
IN YOUR EYES

Sunil Gera

Srishti
PUBLISHERS & DISTRIBUTORS

SRISHTI PUBLISHERS & DISTRIBUTORS
Registered Office: N-16, C.R. Park
New Delhi – 110 019
Corporate Office: 212A, Peacock Lane
Shahpur Jat, New Delhi – 110 049
editorial@srishtipublishers.com

First published by
Srishti Publishers & Distributors in 2015

Dedicated to my mother, Kailash Gera
and father, Sukhdayal Gera.

Introduction

Creative writing comes out of dreams. Dreams originate in childhood and during growing years. The writer could develop a style, web a plot, and turn it into a story when he pens down those dreams. I think only those stories which come out of the heart turn on the readers' imagination, make them excited and compel them to read.

With the medium of storytelling, the writer creates the feeling of spring among the readers, even in their autumns.

Different writers engage readers in different ways. My personal style has been the quest for success for the underprivileged. My main characters have one quality in common – they don't make compromises for their core values. They pass through difficult life situations, but they never give up. Their lives take them through a maze of intricate, unhappy situations, but they always spring back. They are so driven by passion and desires that they choose unconventional paths. They often break rules and social norms to achieve what they want.

Today's readers are well informed and they don't go by just the conventional norms. They also want to know "whys" and they are ready to accept unconventional endings.

There have been many passionate times in my life. I can relate well with my inner conscious quite often when I get carried away by any moving experience. It could be an unexpected good gesture by someone, a touching song, a well directed movie, and just about anything.

I have quite clear memories of those who supported my passion in writing. I would give the first credit to some authors, whose writings moved me. In initial years they were Daphne du Maurier, Jane Austen and Margaret Mitchell.

I loved writing in good natural surroundings such as at Hauz Khas tomb, Nainital, Kanatal, Mussoorie, Simla, Goa and even cities abroad like London, New York, Boston, among others. I could be inspired by any situation or any experience of life.

The first experience of creative writing that I can recollect was an inter-school essay writing competition in Delhi. It was held in Harcourt Butler School and it was in Hindi. Once I got into the mood of writing, my imagination got very vivid and I could write through the entire duration with full concentration.

In my college days, I was very restless due to inner turmoil, a disconnect with the educational system. During those days I was exposed to more authors such as Ayn Rand, Somerset Maugham and Harper Lee.

It took me several decades to discover my real passion. Initially I was not confident, but I learnt through the experiences of others. Many of my doubts got cleared with the passage of time. Many self-help trainers such as Louise Hay, Anthony Robbins, and Stephen Covey were also responsible in making me realize my dream. Their practical guidance was extremely useful.

I am thankful to team Srishti for the publication of this book; Tanvi Bhatt and Dhwani Bhatt from Panache Studio for brand creation and social media publicity; and Gunjan Ahlawat for creating the cover design.

My wife Renu Gera has always provided me a steady support through thick and thin. She has been a friend, guide, critic, editor, storyteller, all rolled in one. She has always kept me very close with my kith and kin by being in regular touch with them. My grandson, Rihaan has been the cynosure of my love and my inspiration all through the writing.

Chapter - I

1

Ranbir got up with a start as the alarm clock rang. He lifted the curtain and peeped outside. It had been raining heavily and the road was shining under the yellow street light. He thought about the escape. He had already packed his suitcases and loaded them in the dicky of the car the previous night.

He had planned to leave Mumbai for the time being and was considering driving to his hometown, Bathinda in Punjab, in his Ambassador. He took a bath and changed into blue jeans, a casual shirt and sneakers. His stay in Mumbai had been tumultuous.

He picked up his hand bag, wallet and the car keys and switched off the electric mains. He had switched off his mobile the previous night itself. He locked the exit door and walked to his car. He could hear the landline phone ringing when he was on his way out. He knew that the call was from Karkhanis. He had not allowed him any peace after the due date of loan repayment. He feared that his henchmen would be outside his door if he stayed any longer.

He settled into the driving seat and drove out of the main gate. The torrential rain had flooded the road. The bylane had the water logging problem, so he maneuvered carefully and approached the main road which was clean and smooth.

Mumbai looked heavenly in the early hours of the day, particularly during the monsoon. His car passed Versova road and he could hear the waves lashing on the sea shore. In half an hour he had cleared Dahisar check post and his car was speeding on the Western Express Highway. The sky had cleared and raindrops were now falling gently. He had come to Mumbai with his dream of producing a film one year back. His film *Aaj Ki Shaam* had been released and had flopped. Only a handful of cine goers came to watch it. The cinema owners decided to stop showing the film after running it for just two days.

Ranbir had himself witnessed near empty cinema houses on Friday and Saturday and he knew that his dream had come to an end.

On the same Friday, KJ's film *Shahanai* had also released. In contrast to his film *Aaj Ki Shaam,* the public was going in hordes to see KJ's film in eight cinema houses. There were bill boards at various strategic locations and the film was being advertised on TV, radio and cinema houses. There was a buzz all over and young and old were talking about its star cast, music and dialogues. The rush had continued on Saturday also.

Ranbir was more scared than dejected. He had borrowed two crores from Karkhanis. He had received all the money in cash. He was supposed to return the money with ten percent interest within three months. The loan tenure had ended two days back. He was supposed to pay back the loan from the collections from the distributors. As per the agreements, they were under no obligation to pay him even a dime now because his film had flopped.

Karkhanis's henchmen had visited his house the previous night. He had a glimpse of them leaving his building from his car. He knew that they would be there the next morning too.

He had come to Mumbai after selling his ancestral land in Bathinda a year back. He had made his film by investing his entire five crores. He had well overshot his budget and after borrowing two crores from Karkhanis, he still had to do without advertising. The cut on the advertising had spelt the death knell for his film. His film, *Aaj Ki Shaam* was released in eight theatres in Mumbai but there were no bill boards, media reviews and interviews to pull the crowds. The critics' review in *Screen*, a film journal was a squib. He had commented about the lead cast, "The heroine was acceptable but the new comer hero lacked expression!"

It was all over as the theatres had stopped showing the film. He had made a bad investment and lost all his capital as well as Karkhanis's loan and he did not know how to repay him.

He had been driving for two hours and he thought of stopping for a while. After driving for a few minutes, he saw a signboard - Hotel Amigo. He went in, freshened himself and ordered coffee and vegetable sandwiches.

When he was back on the road, he thought of the upheavals he had undergone during the production of the film. The distributors had seen the preview and they needed the climax of the film to be shot again and they wanted two item numbers with a lot of skin show to be included. Their specific conditions had to be fulfilled before the film could be released.

He went to the financers to borrow three crores. He could manage to get only two crores from Karkhanis. He also knew that he charged high interest and had the reputation of recovering his money by force. After borrowing at a heavy interest rate, the last three months had been very taxing.

By the time *Aaj Ki Shaam* was completed and released, he had exhausted all the borrowed funds. He was a novice in the field and had made the mistake of ignoring the importance of advertising. In two days, he had lost everything including the borrowed funds. In simple words, he was bankrupt and had no option but to escape from Mumbai.

The drive up to Surat was uneventful. It was around two when he reached Regent Hotel on the highway near Surat. He booked a room and filled the tub with hot water. He took off his clothes and immersed his body in it. The feeling was refreshing and his body seemed rejuvenated. He switched on his mobile and called up Meera.

"Hello, Ranbir. Nice to hear from you."

"Hello Meera!" He spoke with a steady tone.

Meera was the heroine of his film. She had received her full payment in time. She knew that the film had flopped and she understood that as a consequence, her market value would come down. She also realized that it was harder on Ranbir as he had lost all his capital and now owed a big sum to the financer.

"Hello, where are you calling from?" She sounded worried.

"I am at a distributor's office," he lied to cover up his embarrassment.

"There were two calls today. Your financer, Karkhanis was sounding a little rough and wanted to talk to you. The second caller was Suleiman bhai, your distributor from north and east territory. Both said that your mobile was switched off and no one was picking up the landline phone. Suleiman bhai said that collections of the film have been bad. He wanted to get in touch with you."

"Please give me the distributor's number, I shall contact him right away. I will contact Karkhanis too."

Ranbir knew that her sympathies wouldn't help him, so after getting the distributor's number, he said a hurried goodbye and hung up.

He was worried that no matter where he went, Karkhanis would find him. He had no solution to this problem and his mind was blank.

He called up the distributor because he was still his debtor, even though the film had flopped.

"Hey Suleiman bhai, Ranbir speaking. Meera informed me that you had called."

"Yes, Ranbir bhai, the collections for the last two days have been bad. I wanted to can *Aaj Ki Shaam* in the north and east territories also, but there have been good collections in the noon show, probably it was a Sunday."

"That is the first good news I have received in the last three months. What are your plans? Will theatre owners be showing the film in the coming days too?" Ranbir asked hopefully.

"Insha'Allah! They should continue till there are a respectable number of cine-goers. I had received half the payments from theatre owners and they shall pay me the balance if they can run the film for a week." Suleiman gave him a brief.

"Insha'Allah! You may get the crowds in the forthcoming shows too," Ranbir said with some cheer in his voice.

"Suleiman bhai, will you be able to send some payment to me?" Ranbir asked diffidently.

"Yes, if *Aaj Ki Shaam* runs for one week and I get the balance from the theatre owners, I shall send you your full dues of two crores."

His assurance gave Ranbir some solace to be able to deal with the difficult situation facing him.

"Thanks, Suleiman bhai!"

He switched off his mobile, changed into fresh clothes and walked into the bar. He ordered some chilled beer, fish fingers and a green salad.

Sitting in the bar, with no known soul around, he dwelt on his personal life.

The lilting music by Rafi from the film *Baiju Bawara* was playing in the room: *Oh duniya key rakhwale, sun dard bhare mere nare…*

The melody, the words and the high pitch of Mohammed Rafi's voice aptly suited the quagmire in which he found himself. His eyes became moist as he got lost in the music.

He looked at his watch. It was a few minutes before four. He had covered two hundred and seventy kilometres since morning. He went back to the room to get his bag and checked out of the hotel. He wanted to cover another two hundred and fifty kilometres before retiring for the night. He steered his car to NH 8 highway to resume his journey.

"What will I do in Bathinda?" This question occupied his mind. He could set up a dhaba there. He had a smile on his face as he pictured himself serving tasty food and leading a rustic life. In his mind he started visualizing the laid back attitude of the villagers, the rhythm of country music and the folk dances, the smell of earth after a shower and tasty paranthas.

His one problem regarding occupation was solved. The second problem was marriage. Finding a suitable partner would be a tough pursuit but he did not want to delay that any longer as he imagined marrying a simple village belle.

His mood had changed and he was happy that he was going back, even though he had lost all his wealth.

2

Ranbir reached Ahmedabad at 8.30 pm. He decided to check into Hotel Cama, and freshened up before finally switching his phone on again and calling up Meera to know of recent developments.

"Hello Meera, how are you?"

"Hello Ranbir, where are you? I tried to call you up on your mobile and your landline."

"Meera, I am meeting some financers to arrange for some interim finance. I was busy in meetings throughout the day," he lied again.

"Were your meetings successful? Karkhanis sounded very impatient. He was trying to track you. He called me twice after our last telephonic conversation."

"I am sorry, I will call him up immediately."

"By the way, I have two crores in cash with me. If you want you can take it, and pay me back at your convenience."

He was taken aback by Meera's gesture. He tried to appraise his situation in the changed circumstances.

Two persons, Meera and Suleiman, had already given him hope about raising four crores. He owed Karkhanis two crores twenty lakhs, including interest. There was a chance of gains from southern, central, and western territories without Mumbai, overseas territories and video rights as well. He could try to release his film in Mumbai and certain territories after advertising once more. After all, a man was not defeated till he had given up.

"Meera, how can you trust me so much?"

"You have been very fair with everyone. *Aaj Ki Shaam* is a good film; the only flaw is that it has not been advertised. How can you expect public to go to watch a movie that they barely know anything about."

"I am grateful, but I wouldn't need your funds, as I have already lined up a financer."

"Good! Come over sometime. Karim's has opened a branch in Navi Mumbai and we could try their kebabs!"

Ranbir smiled as his tension evaporated.

"Meera, I will come as soon as I get things in order. Your words have given me hope." He disconnected the line on a positive note.

He thought about Karkhanis. In his heart he was afraid of him. He tried a psychological trick. He imagined Karkhanis screaming and threatening him with dire consequences. He transformed him into a court jester in his mind, jumping up and down, yelling and gesticulating. He imagined him wearing red and white clothes with frills, with a conical red cap on his head and his nose painted red. In a few minutes he found that his threats were having the opposite effect on him. He was no longer afraid of him, on the contrary, he was amused.

He dialled Karkhanis's number.

"Oh, you bastard, where are you? You come here and pay me my money otherwise I will send my goons to bump you off." He shouted from the other end, without even hearing a hello from Ranbir.

Ranbir smiled thinking of him as the jester, "Cool off, your threats will not help you to recover your loan."

"You bastard, I will show you who I am.'"

"If you do not want to listen to me, then I am disconnecting the line!"

"Okay, tell me when are you returning my loan?"

Ranbir noted a slight softening in Karkhanis's tone. He answered distinctly, "I will pay you two crores in fifteen days but I am sorry I cannot pay your interest!"

"Why, I have lent you money to earn interest. So I don't care how you pay me. I want my principle as well as interest, not your excuses."

"My film has been canned in Mumbai. I have lost my capital as well as your loan amount. You are lucky that I am still returning your principle."

There was a pause at the other end. Ranbir's bold statement was gradually sinking into his head.

"Fine, give me two crores. And fifteen days mean fifteen days. This is the last time. After that, I will not spare you."

"Okay," Ranbir said and disconnected the phone.

He was happy that he had got the interest waived off from a tough financer and he was relieved that he had got fifteen days to collect the cash from his distributors.

He decided to return to Mumbai to make a second attempt to establish himself in the city of dreams.

3

Ranbir didn't want to drive back. He asked at the reception if he could get a good driver to take his car to Mumbai the next morning. Fifteen minutes later, a decent looking driver approached him. Ranbir readily agreed to the two thousand rupees the driver quoted and gave him the car keys along with one thousand rupees to get the car checked, washed and fuelled up before they started at nine the next morning. That night, he had a sound sleep after a long time.

In the morning, Ranbir had breakfast in the room and checked out. The driver had gotten the car washed and polished, and stood in the porch, waiting for him.

After he was seated in the back seat, the driver switched on the air conditioner and steered the car out of the porch. The car ploughed through heavy traffic till it came to the highway. Ranbir picked up a magazine and leafed through it while his mind was lost in old memories.

Meera walked with steady steps with two books in her hand. She wore a yellow kameez, white churidar and white sandals. It was one of the first few days in college.

College boys, Ranbir and Arun, walked about twenty steps behind her, keeping a watch on her gait.

"She has baby fat on her thighs," Arun said.

Arun was a sophomore in Hindu College. He had a good command over the English language; he had studied in St. Columba's School. He was tall and good looking and he was the son of a diplomat. He wanted to work for an English newspaper after his graduation.

"Meera is in IP College and she is my heartthrob," Ranbir admitted; he was in the first year of law.

Ranbir hadn't thought of the future. He thought that college was the time to enjoy life. He had learnt through his friends that the law course provided admission to Delhi University and it was not demanding. One could take life easy. His father had been the Deputy Commissioner in the Excise department and he had taken early retirement to start his own private practice. He handled government revenue cases. He had made a lot of money under the table while he was still in government service. In those years, he had built a three storied house in Green Park and had bought an office at Tees Hazari near the Civil court.

"Are you going to rag the juniors?"Ranbir asked.

"Oh sure, there will be so much fun today! Officially ragging has been banned, yet there is a lot of fun in the common areas," Arun said.

Meera had reached the bus stand. She was now waiting for the University special bus. Following her, Ranbir and Arun had also reached at the bus stand.

Ranbir and Arun talked at a slightly louder pitch so that she could hear their conversation.

In a few minutes, the University special arrived. All the students boarded the bus. Meera got a window seat, while Arun and Ranbir stood nearby. Though it was public transport, yet it had the glamour of Delhi. There were only students in the bus, apart from the conductor and the driver. Some students were chirpy, while the others either listened to their iPods or looked outside the windows.

Arun resumed the conversation, "Would you like to participate in an inter-college extempore competition?"

"Where?" Ranbir inquired.

"In IP College next Friday!" Arun replied.

Ranbir was interested as Meera was a student there.

"What's the topic?"

"The subjects will be different for different participants. Each participant will get his or her subject only five minutes before his or her turn to speak. The judges will announce the results on the basis of content of the speeches and on the effectiveness of delivery."

"Will you be participating?"

"Yes, besides me, there are two more students from Hindu college."

"I'll speak to our college cultural secretary and check whether I can represent the college," Ranbir said.

Ranbir and his classmate Anil had come to participate in the extempore speech competition at IP College. They were contestants and therefore were respectfully escorted by four girls to the auditorium.

The college had an atmosphere of excitement and fun and gradually the auditorium filled up with the students, the faculty members and the contestants. Ranbir could spot Meera who stood along with two of her friends near the side entrance. He asked Anil to keep his seat reserved and he got up to introduce himself to her. He was sure that as he was a guest participant in her college function, she would consider his direct approach as a friendly gesture.

"Hello, my name is Ranbir." He introduced himself.

"Hello, I am Meera." She replied, smiling.

"We board the bus from the same bus stand in the mornings."

"Yes, I have seen you. It is nice meeting you. Good luck."

Meera was eighteen and quite tall. She had thick black long hair, smooth fair skin and a lovely face. Her eyes were bright and she had a playful smile.

The contest was well-organized. Ranbir performed well and won a prize.

Meera came to congratulate him after the prize distribution. They continued their tete-a-tete during the snacks session after the contest. He learnt that she was a student of Social Sciences and she lived with her mother in Safdarjung Development Area.

After the introduction, they met again at the Hauz Khas Village near her home soon after.

Meera was beautiful. She came dressed in a white cotton frock. The helm of her frock was four inches above her knees, and Ranbir noticed her shapely legs. She wore high heels, which made her look quite tall.

Ranbir held her hand and looked into her eyes. She felt a warm sensation going through her hand to her entire body. She lowered her eyelids and blushed.

He asked gently, "Do you like me holding your hand?"

She still looked down but raised her eyebrows slightly and nodded in affirmation.

He touched her lips with the index finger of his other hand. A tremor passed through her body. She softly moved her head back and tried to disengage her hand from his hold.

"Do you want me to leave?" He playfully questioned her.

"No, let's talk!" she responded.

"Alright, would you come with me for a picnic on Sunday?" he asked.

"Where?"

"*We will go to Badhkhal Lake.*"

"*How?*"

"*I have a Bullet.*"

"*Okay, you can pick me up at nine,*" she replied excitedly.

He was delighted that she wanted to ride on his bike. He was convinced that she had liked his company; he slowly lifted her hand and planted a kiss on it. She smiled and withdrew her hand.

They met at nine in the morning outside her home. The weather was very pleasant. She looked dazzling in her jeans and long boots. She wore a purple top and a black scarf. He kick started the bike and sat on the rider's seat. She sat behind on the pillion with her legs on either side. She hugged him tightly as he moved the bike. He drove leisurely to New Friends Colony crossing while she had her hands around him with her torso against his back.

She remarked, "*You are going so slowly!*"

He accelerated upon hearing her say it so playfully. He balanced the bike with his left hand and with the right hand, held her right palm and brought it to his lips. Although he brought his right hand back to the handle, she let her hand remain on his lips. He was driving fast, gliding past the traffic on Mathura road.

They ate snacks at Haldiram's and went boating at Badhkhal Lake. She told him that she wanted to be a model or an actress. He was quite surprised to learn about her interests. That was the first time Ranbir thought about his own career. He imagined his future in film making. He learnt through her that it required a minimum of five crores to make a commercial film.

In the afternoon they watched a film at Neelam theatre. They had a good outing that day.

Back home, Ranbir asked his father if he could give him five crores after his studies as he wanted to produce a film in Mumbai. His father was not amused and got worried when he learnt about his son's wayward interests. He decided to send him to his elder brother in Bathinda, where they had farms. He could work there. He couldn't disobey his father and left for his village.

He completed his graduation in Arts through a correspondence course in the Indira Gandhi National Open University and worked in the farms. About five years later, he learnt of his father's demise. He and his elder brother drove to Delhi to perform the last rites.

They sold off their Delhi properties. He also went to Meera's house where he learnt from her mother that after her graduation, she had got a good break in modelling and acting in films, and had shifted to Mumbai. Her first film was about to be released in a month's time. Ranbir once again got excited about moving to Mumbai to become a film producer. On his return, he discussed his idea with his brother.

His brother agreed to buy his share of inheritance and he gave him five crores. His elder brother thought it would be best if Ranbir followed his dreams.

Ranbir left for Mumbai and rented a two bedroom apartment in Versova. He opened a bank account in the neighbourhood and made some contacts in the film industry. Soon he started working on his debut film.

The car had reached a toll booth and Ranbir's chain of thoughts got interrupted. He made a small conversation with the driver and then went back to his thoughts. He wondered why he didn't feel as relaxed always as he was feeling that day.

They had a lunch break for half-an-hour near Surat. They had another break for tea and snacks at Vasai and finally the car reached his apartment at 8 pm. He paid the driver his due, and also a tip of two hundred rupees.

4

Meera completed her graduation in Arts from IP college, Delhi. She had decided to become a model. She was picked up by Hindustan Thompson for a modelling assignment which took her to Mumbai.

She gained fame and consequently got a lead role in a Bollywood film. She became successful and made a good fortune within two years. She bought a penthouse in Navi Mumbai and decorated it tastefully. She invested her money in gold ornaments, and also bought an Altis Corolla and a Ford Transit van.

She learnt from her mother that Ranbir had visited her house in Delhi and planned to come to Mumbai.

Meera received Ranbir's call about a month later.

She was happy to hear from him and they fixed up a meeting at the Samovar restaurant.

Samovar was a place of rendezvous for art lovers. The restaurant had a great ambience because it was housed in Jehangir Art Gallery itself. In earlier times, even MF Husain, Jatin Das and the likes were often seen there.

Ranbir found Meera to be as beautiful as she had been during the beginning of college life. She had added poise and glamour. Though she was a known model and an actor, she was unassuming with him.

"I have decided to become a film producer. I have received all my inheritance in cash and I have come here to make my debut film. I have selected a script and my debut film is to be called Aaj Ki Shaam. *I want you to be the female lead actor in my film."*

She looked very enthusiastic, "Oh fine, I agree. I am sure the script will be good."

Since Meera and Ranbir had shared a special relationship, they had a good chemistry as heroine and director on the sets.

They worked hard as professionals and finally Aaj Ki Shaam *got completed.*

Meera had got her payments in time. She was not involved with the commercial and marketing aspects of the film, therefore she was unaware about the acuteness of Ranbir's financial problem.

Ranbir had to release his film without advertising due to shortage of funds.

Meera got busy with her next modelling assignment for Boroline skin cream after the release of the film. However, she had a break of seven days before her outdoor shoot at Kodiakanal. She called her friend Radha who was a creative artist in the Everest Advertising Company.

"Radha, let us go to Bangkok for four days," Meera proposed.

"Meera, you must be crazy to suggest a holiday. I am totally immersed in my work for the cover of *Cosmopolitan* magazine. There is no respite till the May issue gets printed," Radha expressed her dissent.

Meera made the next call to her cousin Sunanda. She had completed her MBBS from Kasturba Medical College. She had applied for an internship in three well-known hospitals in Mumbai and she was waiting for the results. She was confident of being selected in at least one of them.

"Hey, it's wonderful to hear from you after a long time," Sunanda said.

Meera said, "My film is completed and it is having an average run in other parts of the country and overseas, but unfortunately it has flopped in Mumbai. I am free for seven days till my outdoor shoot for a modelling assignment starts. I thought we could go for a game of bowling at Seven Seas.

Sunanda replied, "I am game. Can you pick me up? You must come up. Ma will be very happy to meet you."

Meera agreed and fixed the meeting for eleven.

She asked her driver to get her Altis Corolla ready and instructed the driver to raise the tinted window panes so that she could not be identified during the drive.

The car reached Sunflower Building, where Sunanda lived, in forty-five minutes. Meera asked the driver to wait in the parking lot and went up to meet Sunanda and her mother. As soon as she rang the apartment bell, she heard Mozo, the Dachshund barking. Sunanda opened the door and he also came along to welcome her.

Sunanda remarked, "Lovely, I was about to call you, wondering if you had changed your mind."

"I am sorry I am late. The traffic's terrible," Meera replied with a smile.

"It is fine," Sunanada said and held her hand gently.

Meera walked ahead to meet Sunanda's mother, who was in the kitchen making some tea for them.

"Hello Mami, how are you?" she said with a lot of affection.

"Hello Meera, it doesn't seem as though we stay in the same city. You come to meet us after months!" Mami made her usual complaint.

All of them sat down in the drawing room and sipped tea and devoured the dhokla and khakhara.

Meera and Sunanda got up to go to the bowling alley.

As Sunanda joined Meera on the back seat of the car, she asked her, "Hey, how is Ranbir? Will he be able to recover his investment?"

"Our film is having an average run in rest of the country and in the overseas market. Unfortunately, it hasn't done too well in Mumbai. He will just recover his investment, I think." She answered her, showing a lot of concern.

"Now as the film has been completed and released, will you guys be together or would you be going your separate ways?" Sunanda wanted to dig deeper about their relationship.

"I have invited him informally, but it seems he is busy sorting out the financial problems. Guess he'll meet me after some time," Meera replied candidly.

"When are you expected to get the communication from the hospitals?" Meera asked Sunanda.

"I expect the response from KEM this week and Bombay hospital and Breach Candy hospitals by next week."

"So, if you get admission in all the three, which one you would choose?

"My first choice would be Breach Candy!"

They were busy yakking about their lives, while their car reached Seven Seas.

Sunanda paid for the bowling tickets. There were six bowling alleys. One of the alleys got free in fifteen minutes and they got their turn for an hour.

It was a neck to neck fight. In the end, Sunanda's score was 168 and Meera's score was 155. Both enjoyed the game thoroughly.

They went to Khyber restaurant for lunch. They ordered beer with seekh kebabs. The main course included tandoori chicken, makhani daal, raita and nans.

Meera treated Sunanda with Blueberry cheesecake ice cream at Baskin Robbins before dropping her home.

5

Ranbir waited for seven days for the debtors to send him his payments. He couldn't wait any longer and called up Suleiman first.

"Hello, I am Ranbir. You had promised to send me my payment."

"Hello Ranbir bhai, I had been out of station. I will call up the theatre owners and shall give you the reply within two to three days."

He was quite disappointed at Suleiman's casual approach, however, he maintained his cool and politely asked him, "My requirement is rather urgent. Can you please send me the amount by tomorrow?"

"Ranbir bhai, I am sorry but it will take some time."

"Suleiman bhai, you said that you have got half your payment already. Why don't you send me half of my payment now and send the rest in two-three days."

"Okay, I will call you up later," Suleiman replied and hung up.

Ranbir called up his other distributors – southern, central, western region besidesMumbai, overseas territories, TV channels and video rights but he couldn't get them on line. He simply left messages for them.

His last date to pay Karkhanis was only seven days away. He hoped that the situation would change for the better.

He needed a distraction from the anxiety. He called up Meera for some respite.

"Hi, nice to hear from you; want to try Karims' kebabs?" she asked cheerfully.

"Sure, I will be at your place in two hours." He said briefly and disconnected the line.

He knew her apartment in Navi Mumbai as he had dropped her once on the way back after a shooting schedule in Khandala. However, it was the first time that he was visiting her. He had always had feelings for her, but he couldn't say the words when he was in her company.

On the way, he stopped his car near the florist and bought a bouquet of roses.

Belverde was a new eight-storeyed building on the sea side with gardens in the front and back. She lived in the penthouse. When he reached her apartment, the maid opened the door. He sat on a sofa and was served water. Meera entered after about five minutes. She looked fresh in a green sari, diamond earrings and gold bangles adding to her charm.

Ranbir smiled and got up to welcome her. He gave her the roses, put his arm around her waist and gently pecked her on her cheek. She also smiled and bent her face a little forward. She accepted the flowers, inhaled the fragrance and neatly placed them in a vase. She sat on the sofa, right opposite him.

They were meeting after a gap of a month. In between they had spoken only three times.

Meera saw that Ranbir had lost some weight. He wore a cotton cream coloured half sleeved shirt and light brown cotton trousers with matching dark brown leather shoes. His hair was neatly blown back.

"You look smart!" She complimented him.

"Thanks and you look ravishing!" He smiled.

"What would you care to have? Tea or coffee? The kebabs are on the way."

"Tea and kebabs will be a good combination," he replied.

"How are the results of *Aaj Ki Shaam*?"

"The film is drawing half/full houses in other territories except in Mumbai where it has flopped. But the payments have yet to come. The distributors are delaying it."

"What do they say?" she asked.

"It seems they want to recover their investment first and then they want to pay me from the surplus," he replied morosely.

"That is not fair. Shouldn't they send you at least part of your payment?" she asked with concern in her voice.

"I think the payments will come through a week or two weeks later. These distributors have been in business for a long time," he said optimistically.

"In case you have any urgency, I can give you two crores," she extended her help once again.

"Thanks very much for your help, I don't need it right now. In case I need it in the future, then I shall ask for it." He was really touched by her offer.

The maid entered and informed her that the kebabs were ready and they could proceed to the dining room.

Meera guided Ranbir to the dining room. The table was laid out with mutton tikkas, chicken seekh kebabs and fish tikkas. In addition, there were salads, mint chutney, mayonnaise, mustard sauce and tea. She first served him and then helped herself. Both were pretty hungry and they devoured all the items.

After they were through with the food, they returned to the drawing room. Meera was unaware of the seriousness of his financial problem, since he had assured her that he had no desperate pressure for the funds. He, on the other hand, didn't want her to be burdened with his problem. He valued their friendship; he didn't want to complicate it with the exchange of money.

She had a special liking for him, appreciated his integrity, and found him very different from the other producers. She admired his ability to invest everything he owned to make his film and he had always been fair to his team. Once he settled the terms with them, he strictly adhered to his commitments. Till the first preview of the film for the distributors, he hadn't needed to borrow any money, so his team got their full dues. Thereafter the distributors had asked for certain changes which led to his borrowing from the financer.

She asked him to relax on the armed chair and went to play some music on her music system. She played a song from Aamir Khan's film *Fanaa*:

Mere haath mein tera haath ho, sari jannate mere saath hon; tu jo paas ho phir kya yeh jahan, tere pyaar mein ho jaun fanaa....

Both Ranbir and Meera sat together listening to the music, immersed in nostalgia of their college days.

After some time, Ranbir got up to leave.

"I better leave; it has been lovely meeting you and enjoying your hospitality."

"Do drop in again. Take care."

Meera and Ranbir held hands as they walked to the lift. He held her by her waist, she brought her face closer and he pecked her gently below her ear.

As Meera went back to her penthouse, Ranbir drove towards Palm Beach. He was happy that he always followed his instincts rather than the safe path. He could have accepted her loan and could have relieved himself from Karkhanis's pressure. His inner voice prompted him to keep his relationship with her out of his business problems.

Once his car reached Palm Beach, he parked it on the side and walked on the damp sand for about two hundred meters. He sat down on a rock and concentrated on his inner conscious. The sea was calm and the sky a serene blue.

He found nature in its full glory and he could feel his inner consciousness being one with it. He felt that he was not limited by his body or his problems. He believed that everything in the world happened with a purpose.

He thought about Meera. She was beautiful and successful and she cared for him. He thought that even this reward alone more than compensated for all the problems he had faced in his venture.

He thought about the experience that he had gained about the art of film making, which was a big reward in itself. A year back when he had come to Mumbai, he had only his capital and his ambition to produce a film. Only with experience he got a better understanding about his strengths and weaknesses. He was sure that in case he got another opportunity of making a film, he would do a fairly good job. He realized that he had learnt a great deal from his mistakes.

6

"Hello, Karkhanis. I have been trying but there could be a delay of a few days." Ranbir said tersely.

Karkhanis was upset, and said in anger, "Listen, I am not interested in your problems, your due date passed a fortnight back."

"Look, you are in the business of financing and I am in the business of film making. We may meet each other after this transaction also," Ranbir replied without showing any nervousness.

"I am not interested in lending to a flop producer. You are not paying my interest also. In fact, I will be losing money even if I get my capital back."

By that time Karkhanis's voice pitch had come down by a few decibels.

"I wanted to inform you that I am doing my best and I am after all my distributors to pay my dues. I cannot, however, be rough with them as you are with me."

"You cannot call my behaviour with you rough because you do not know what I do with other defaulters. It's only because you have been calling me instead of my calling you that I am not rough," Karkhanis barked before he disconnected the line.

He was feeling relieved that he could buy some more time from him so that he could follow up with his distributors.

He picked up the phone and called up Suleiman, "Hello, I need to meet you in Delhi tomorrow."

"Ranbir bhai, you are welcome. What time you want to meet me?"

He was surprised by the pleasantness with which Suleiman accepted his proposal. He added, "Tomorrow two o'clock in your office."

"Fine, I will wait for you."

Ranbir disconnected the line and called his travel agent to book his flight ticket for the next morning.

The flight arrived at Indira Gandhi International Airport at 12.30 pm.

He freshened himself at the airport and left for Suleiman's office situated at Jhandewalan. When he walked towards the reception, it was two minutes to two. He asked for Suleiman bhai.

Suleiman himself came to receive him at the reception and he took Ranbir to his room.

"I have lunch ready for both of us, we can first eat," Suleiman proposed.

He was not hungry, yet he agreed. They shifted to an adjacent room which was connected to the pantry. A waiter in white uniform served them the food. They had Rogan josh, nans, chicken biryani and onion raita. The food was cooked well and it was hot.

After lunch, they came back to Suleiman's room. Suleiman asked the waiter to serve them tea.

Suleiman bhai said, "Ranbir bhai, in the final count, your film has done an average run. In the last two weeks the collection from north are five crores and from east are five-and-a-half crores. Therefore, I can offer you your entire dues of two crores."

Ranbir was pleased with him and he said, "That is good news. How are you going to pay it?"

Suleiman bhai replied, "I will give you a check of one crore and fifty lakhs and fifty lakhs in cash."

Ranbir was very happy but he did not show his excitement and said, "That will be fine."

Suleiman gave instructions to his accountant on the intercom. Within ten minutes, the accountant had got the check and cash ready.

Ranbir was through with the meeting. He was eager to leave Suleiman's office and heaved a sigh of relief.

Ranbir decided to go back to the airport. He had an open Jet Airways ticket. He showed it at the counter to check for the first return flight. He could get a seat in a flight which was to take off within an hour. He was very happy with the turn of events. These two crores were his first collection. After spending seven crores – comprising his capital as well as the loan amount – getting the first payment of two crores was more than welcome. It really called for a celebration.

He called up Meera. "Hi, I have good news to share. I have received my first payment of two crores from Suleiman bhai." He mentioned to her excitedly.

"That is wonderful news! What about your other distributors, when are they making the payments?"

"I will be after them from tomorrow onwards."

"You should pay personnel visits to them as well," she instructed him pleasantly.

He thanked her for her suggestion before disconnecting the line.

He thought of returning the entire amount of two crores to Karkhanis as soon as the check was cleared.

7

Ranbir's flight landed at Chhatrapati Shivaji International Airport at 8 pm.

Meera was at the airport carrying a bouquet of gladiolas for him. They hugged and lightly kissed each other.

"Hey, congratulations! That was a fast job."

"Thanks, luckily Suleiman is a good distributor. He was ready to pay my full amount."

They went to the car parking, Meera handed him the car keys and Ranbir sat on the driver's seat. He steered the car out of the parking towards Linking Road.

Meera and Ranbir stopped at Barista. She wanted to spend some time with Ranbir before her modelling shoot.

"Pass me your packet."

Ranbir took out his Wills Classic packet and lighter from his pocket and handed them over to Meera.

She lit the cigarette and drew a deep puff.

She exhaled slowly and remarked, "Man, these shifts are killing. I am quitting before the month end."

Ranbir placed the order for two Cappuccinos.

"What will you do then?"

"I will wait for you to make your next movie."

Ranbir smiled and quipped smilingly, "I don't think you would have the patience to wait. You can call up KJ; he is interested in a heroine for his new film."

"I am going to a dance party at 11 Echoes on Friday evening. Can you be my partner?" Meera asked.

"I am sorry, I don't think so," Ranbir replied.

Meera smiled; she knew that Ranbir loved dancing and he required a little persistence to commit himself.

After dropping Ranbir home, Meera drove to Filmistan studios for the shoot.

8

Ranbir called, "Karkhanis, I want to meet you."

"What time?"

"In one-and-a-half hours from now."

"Are you coming with the money?"

"Yes."

"You can come now as I am in the office."

After the brief conversation, he picked up the suitcase which contained two crores in cash.

He carefully kept the suitcase in the dicky of his car and drove the vehicle to Opera House. He parked his vehicle in the parking of Panchratna building and took the lift to Karkhanis's office on the tenth floor.

He was escorted by an armed guard to Karkhanis's room. Karkhanis wore a silk kurta and pyjama. He had a thick gold chain around his neck, wore a red teeka on his forehead, and his hair was oily and short. He called his assistant on the intercom.

"How much cash have you brought?" He came to point straightaway.

"Two crores."

Karkhanis looked relieved and he asked his assistant to count the cash.

After the cash was handed over to the cashier, Karkhanis asked, *"Chai peeso!"*

"*Saru.*" Ranbir nodded.

In two minutes, both were served tea in small stainless steel glasses.

"*Kya kare hamara dhandha hi aisa hai, zor zabardasti ke bina kaam nahin chalta. Maaf karna agar hamse koi bhool chook ho gayi ho,*" Karkhanis said in a friendly tone.

"*Koi baat nahin, meri bhi galti hai,*" Ranbir politely replied.

Ranbir and Karkhanis bade each other goodbye and he left with a sigh of relief. He was empty handed but at least he didn't owe anything to anyone.

Naaz, an Iranian beer bar was around the corner. He walked inside and ordered a chilled London Pilsner beer. A waiter served him peanuts in a small bowl and brought a beer bottle and a glass mug.

Ranbir took a swig and thought about his further course of action. The beer had a cooling effect on him. He finished the remaining beer, the peanuts, paid the bill and tipped the waiter. He walked back to his car and drove back to his residence, whistling on the way:

"*Chala jata hoon kisi ki dhun me, dharakte dil ke tarane liye...*"

9

Ranbir made phone calls to three of his distributors, and to his dismay, all of them disconnected his calls. He regarded the payment follow up as the most loathsome of all jobs.

He had also learnt that following up required a lot of patience, and giving vent to frustrations meant only trouble. Therefore the only recourse left was to wait and watch.

He had a strong wish to produce his next film within a year. The film industry was an unregulated industry and due to this reason, the green horns had no access to bank finance. He could begin only if he received all his dues from his distributors. His whole day went in just fretting about cash flow problems.

He had uneasy sleep but when he got up the next morning, he tried to be in a better frame of mind. His mood improved dramatically when he received Meera's call.

"Ranbir, please come over for lunch if you're free."

"Oh, you are back from your Kodaikanal assignment? I will be at your place at one if that is okay."

"Perfect. See you!" She said cheerfully and disconnected the line.

He took a bath and got dressed. He drove his car leisurely and on the way, bought a bouquet of red roses. On reaching, he lovingly handed over the bouquet to her. She brought it close to her face and inhaled deeply the scent of the roses. He put his arms around her waist and kissed her on the cheek. She closed her eyes to savour the moment. She looked radiant in a light green salwar, kameez and white duppatta.

With his arm around her, he was once again in an optimistic mood. He announced his next project, "I am making another film and I request your acceptance for the female lead role."

"Oh, that is great. What will be the theme of the film?" she asked excitedly.

"A love story!"

"Who will be the hero of the film?"

"Not the last one, that is for sure, but it is too early to confirm that."

She said enthusiastically, "Yes, it is fine with me! When can you show me the script?"

"I think I will be able to get the script ready within a month and we can start shooting in about two months." He said that with a lot of confidence. He overlooked his financial challenges and he dreamt against all odds.

"After all, life was too short to be wasted and to be afraid!" he thought.

She had made the lunch all by herself. There were boti kebabs, keema matar, makhani daal, aloo gobhi and rice.

They sat at the dining table, helped themselves while the maid served them hot rotis. They had ras malai for dessert.

"You are an excellent cook!" He complimented her.

She looked happy while explaining. "I tried out some recipes from a book by Neeta Mehta and with practice, my cooking has improved."

They got up and walked to the balcony. The sky was clear and the sea offered a panoramic view. He loved her and he found total happiness in her company. He wanted to do the best for her.

Ranbir was sure that she loved him too and if he proposed for marriage, she would most likely accept him. However, the truth stared him in the face. He was a struggling producer and she was a successful star. She already possessed wealth, while he was an upstart. He could become successful but for that he would have to wait.

He drew her close, cupped her face in his palms and lowered his head to kiss her. She responded with pleasure and they locked their lips for a passionate kiss. They stood there enigmatically feeling each other's heartbeats.

He avoided further closeness as he reflected on his financial challenges. He had to overcome many hurdles. He apologized for his hurried departure, "I must leave now, as I need to meet some of my contacts for the next film."

She understood and did not press him to stay longer. She unclasped his hand as they parted. She looked forlorn as he waved goodbye.

10

Ranbir drove to Bandra and visited his distributor of video rights. The office was on the third floor and there was a meeting going on. The operator asked his name, the purpose of his visit and then asked him to wait at the reception.

He picked up one of the film magazines from the table and leafed through it. He was feeling very uneasy as the distributor seemed lax towards fulfilling his obligations. He was supposed to make a payment of one crore. Though it had been over one month from the date of release of the videos in the markets, he had not sent a rupee.

The operator got a message on the intercom and she asked him to go into the distributor's room. He entered the room which was dimly lit and it was quite cold. A wallpaper showing a waterfall covered the background and the hidden lights accentuated the picture.

Ramji sat behind a large teak wood table on a cushioned swivel chair.

He was over forty, with a paunch. He was balding and had cold drooping eyes. He slightly raised himself from the swivel chair and extended a limp hand towards him. Ranbir also extended his hand at the same time. He touched Ranbir's hand for a moment while looking away. Ranbir occupied one of the guests' chairs.

Ramji waited for him to broach the subject. He seemed to be unaware of the issue. Ranbir was tense yet he smiled and stated, "Hello, Ramji bhai. I had tried to call you up a few times, but I think you were busy. I was passing this way, so I took a chance, hoping to meet you."

Ramji acknowledged by nodding and then called for the peon. He looked up towards him and asked, "What will you have, tea or coffee?"

Ranbir replied automatically, "Tea!"

Instantly he regretted it as he was reminded of one of his experienced friend's gospels, "When you go for collection and the debtor party offers you tea or coffee, that means the party would merely indulge in the formalities instead of making the payment."

Ramji looked at the peon and asked him to bring two cups of tea.

"There is a spate of new releases, especially KJ's *Shahanai* and therefore the demand for DVDs of your film is lukewarm. We release all our DVDs on credit. We have started getting part of the outstanding but it will take time for the realization of the full payment." He tried to justify the delay.

The peon brought two glasses of water, two cups of tea and a plate of biscuits.

Ranbir said, "I am starting my new film and for that purpose I need the funds rather urgently. I was hoping you could release fifty percent of my dues immediately and the balance fifty percent in one month's time."

"The market is very tight; we are not getting our dues from all the territories. I can release the payment only after I realize my dues. I think you will have to wait for some time," Ramji said mechanically.

"Please tell me, how long do I have to wait?"

"I can't say but may be around two months."

Ranbir felt disappointed with his attitude, yet he maintained his patience as he had no choice. Ramji spoke about the liquidity crunch in the market for a few more minutes and then Ranbir bade him goodbye.

Ranbir got up but avoided the hand shake this time. He left his office and walked back to his car unhappy.

11

Ranbir realized that there was a difference between the way he dealt with his creditors and the way his distributors dealt with him. He always planned his finances and paid his parties in time, whereas his distributors did not discharge their obligations as carefully. He realized that it would take a long time for the funds to show up. He also feared that the inflow would be scattered over a long span. He was sure that he could not launch another film with irregular cash flow. His only option was to try for private finance with the loan sharks. He chewed over the situation for one full evening and night.

He called up Karkhanis at eleven next day.

"Hello, Karkhanis bhai!"

"Ranbir bhai, *kem chho?*"

"Maja ma chhe!"

Karkhanis gave a pause for him to state the purpose of the phone call.

"I am starting my next film and I need finance for the same." He said expectantly.

Karkhanis knew that Ranbir by now was an experienced film maker and he could be trusted.

"How are the collections for your first film?"

"I have almost broken even. I have yet to collect five crore rupees as outstanding from the distributors."

"What are the delays due to?"

"My distributors say that the collections from theatre owners are slow. Probably they want to recover their investment first and then they want to pay me from the surplus."

"What is your requirement?"

"Seven crores."

"You will have to mortgage all the rights of your next film to me. I can loan you five crores seventy lakhs against that. I will charge two percent per month interest in advance. I can loan you the amount for six months only."

"Okay, when can I come over?"

"You can come tomorrow morning at 10.30."

Ranbir realized that he was perspiring due to the risk involved. He thought about the implications of the default in repayment in case his next film bombed at the box office. He shrugged his shoulders and said to himself, "I am thankful to God for giving me the solution; I can start my new film now."

He called up the script writer, who lived at Paidhuni in Mumbai.

"Hello Varun, how are you?"

"I am fine. Good to hear from you."

"I want you to work on a script for a love story."

"I have a very good script ready. If you want we can meet in the evening. I can read the highlights of the script to you."

"Let's meet at Natraj, Marine Drive at six in the evening."

"Okay."

They met at a bar and occupied a side table from where they had a clear view of cars zipping past Marine Drive and the vast ocean beyond. The bar was comfortably air conditioned and noise free because of the glass windows. They ordered Glenlivet scotch and prawns.

Varun had given it a working title *Aandhiyan*. He gave a brief about the script and read some highlights. They also discussed about the cast, music, cinematography and the climax.

Ranbir liked the story and both settled on ten lakh rupees as the fee for the script.

Ranbir suggested some changes in the script and gave a token of one lakh towards the advance. Varun said he'd incorporate the changes and promised to hand over a soft copy and a hard copy within a fortnight.

12

Ranbir's meeting at Karkhanis office went on for over two hours. An agreement was drafted between their companies, in which he mortgaged all the rights of his new film and he got a loan of about five crores seventy lakhs for a period of six months. He was disbursed only five crores and the remaining amount was deducted in advance towards interest for six months.

Ranbir realized that he had not only invested his inheritance of five crores in film production but taken a further loan of five crores and seventy lakhs. He had to collect his outstanding amount of five crores from his distributors and he had yet to produce and sell his second film. He was confident of making a memorable film but he was worried about the collections from his distributors. He decided not to allow uncertainties to cloud his thinking.

Ranbir wanted to shoot a dance for the launch ceremony of his new film, *Aandhiyan*. He signed up Shailendra as the song writer, Saroj as choreographer, Ravi as music director, Vani as singer, Fali Mistry as cameraman, Rajat as set designer and Dolly as makeup artist. He booked the venue at Film City at Goregaon and ordered for the preparations of the set. He planned to sign up Sanjay as the hero on the day of launch.

On the day of the muhurat, his team – including the heroine, script writer, female singer, song writer, cameraman, music director, choreographer, set designer, make up man, dance artists, technical assistants and Sanjay as the prospective hero of the film – gathered on the set.

Meera was dressed in a saffron lehenga and duppatta with a green choli. Her long tresses were neatly entwined with a string of marigolds. She wore a necklace of red beads, accentuating her full bosom. She was bare footed and her feet were artistically decorated with henna. Ranbir as the director gave the clap and in the presence of the team, Meera gave an artistic performance under the direction of the music director and choreographer. Ranbir signed up Sanjay in the male lead of the film and gave him an advance of ten lakhs. The full team celebrated the launch of *Aandhiyan* with laddoos, tea and samosas on the set.

Meera and Sanjay had seen each other in films earlier but they met for the first time, Meera, Sanjay and Varun spent some time to discuss the script. Ranbir sat with Ravi, Fali, Shailendra, Rajat, Saroj and Vani for a small tete-a-tete. The dance artists, the technical assistants and make up man made the third group and enjoyed a light banter. Each member of the team looked happy and committed. They finally dispersed after the ceremony.

Meera had changed into a suit. Ranbir walked with her to the car park to see her off. Initially they walked side by side but as soon as they reached a secluded stretch, they came closer. They stopped under a banyan tree and he put his right hand behind her head and brought her face close to kiss her. He got the scent of marigolds. She responded lovingly.

"I was dancing only for you," she said softly in his ears.

"Yours was an inspirational dance." He complimented her.

He added, "Our film will be a memorable love story!"

She looked into his eyes. She could feel a sense of pride and determination in his words.

"Last time we missed out on public relations and promotion. We must use the media this time," she said.

"Of course. Where do we start?"

"You can officially announce the launch of our film, *Aandhiyan* and invite a dignitary and the media for dinner.

She added, "Come for dinner tonight and we could discuss this."

He nodded happily. He was delighted to see her commitment. He knew that the start of the film had been successful.

He remembered his brother's pet quote, "Well begun is half done!"

They had reached her Ford Transit van. The driver promptly opened rear left door. They waved goodbye to each other. He went back to the set to make some on the spot payments and to wind up. His launch, advance payments, cost of set, decorations and various other expenses had already touched seventy lakhs.

He left the set at four in the evening and steered his Ambassador home. It was five and he decided to take a nap. He got up after an hour, took a bath and changed into casuals. He went down to his car and drove out of the complex. On the way he stopped to buy a bouquet of roses for Meera.

13

When Ranbir reached the apartment and pressed the bell, the door was opened by a girl in her early twenties.

She smiled and introduced herself, "Hi I am Sunanda, and I am Meera's cousin."

Ranbir acknowledged her greeting with a smile and shook her hand. "Hello, I am Ranbir."

"Yes, I know you are the producer and director of Meera's films." She mentioned smilingly, "Meera is getting ready and she will be with us in another five minutes."

"It is alright."

He was feeling self conscious in the presence of a young woman whom he had met unexpectedly.

He started talking to break the ice, "What do you do?"

"I am a doctor. An intern at Breach Candy Hospital."

"Well, that is great. It's one of the toughest jobs."

She pleasantly acknowledged his compliment and added, "That is true for most doctors who like their profession and are empathetic towards the patients. I was having long working hours the whole week, therefore I took off early today and decided to meet Meera. It is our first meeting after I got the internship."

Meera entered the drawing room in a pink salwar-kameez. She looked beautiful as she smiled and came forward to greet him.

He got up and picked up the bouquet of red roses and handed it to her.

"I am sorry for the delay. I hope you would have introduced yourselves. Sunanda is my cousin and also my school friend."

Sunanda said, "Yes, we just introduced ourselves!"

Meera asked, "Would you care for some champagne? I have a bottle from Bordeaux, France in my fridge."

Both of them approved cheerfully and Meera brought three goblets and the champagne bottle in a tray and placed it on the centre table.

They raised their goblets, cheered and sipped.

"Cheers to Ranbir for launching his second film, *Aandhiyan* today!" Meera announced.

"Cheers to Meera and Sunanda, Meera as the heroine of the film and Sunanda as the new intern!" he added.

They walked to the dining room and sat around the dining table. They helped themselves to chicken chunks, fish fingers and green salad.

"Let us all put our minds together to think about ways to promote the new film." Meera opened up the discussion.

"*Aandhiyan* is a love story... it is a tragedy," Ranbir briefed Sunanda about the theme of the film.

"You can release the music about a month before the release of the film. The music should be released on a few popular FM channels," Meera suggested.

"Ranbir should have interviews on popular TV channels around the date of the release," Sunanda suggested.

"There should be hoardings of the film in all the major cities where the film gets released." He also pitched in.

Ranbir realized that this kind of advertising would mean an additional budget of at least three crores. Thus the total cost of the film would touch ten crores. He thought that overall he might have to take a loan of about five crores even after recovering all the dues of his last film. His experience of the first release had taught him the importance of advertising and promotion, therefore, he didn't flinch at the amount.

Meera asked Sunanda, "Can you arrange for a chief guest for the launch of *Aandhiyan*?"

"With our efforts and contacts, that should not be very difficult. But I think all the publicity which would be generated by the launch at this stage would be forgotten by the time the film gets released. This expense can be avoided."

Ranbir was also averse to kowtowing the bigwigs and he considered it to be an avoidable expense. Meera also agreed that a formal launch by a VIP would not have a direct bearing on the popularity of the film at the time of its release, which would take place a year later. All three agreed to drop the formal launch.

While they were discussing, the maid served them dinner. Meera had made the main dish, mutton do pyaza and the salad herself. Her maid cooked the rest of the sumptuous meal, which was duly followed by a delightful ice cream.

A lot of ideas were pooled in. While looking at the impact of public relations and advertising, they kept in mind the aam aadmi's perspective.

Sunanda was the first to look at her watch. "Oh, it is eleven; I must go as I have to leave for the hospital at six in the morning."

Ranbir also mentioned, "Yes, I didn't realize that we had full two hours of discussion."

Meera thanked both of them for their visit. They got up and she walked with them to the porch.

Sunanda had come in her Altis with her driver. She shook hands with Ranbir and hugged Meera goodbye.

Meera and Ranbir walked to the parking up to his Ambassador. They kissed each other before he drove off. He thought that it had been a very romantic and productive day. He savoured the memories of his kisses with Meera and the company of the new friend, Sunanda.

14

Ranbir was passionate about his new film and on the way home called up Sanjay, "Hello, I am glad that you had accepted lead actor's role at such short notice and have given long dates to help complete the film in ten months."

"I am thankful to you that you had the script and other major elements of the film ready. You took just two meetings to sign me up and pay me the advance. I like your professional attitude," he replied.

"I called you up to say that we need to discuss about the film. Let's meet at Flora at Worli for lunch tomorrow?"

"Sounds great. See you."

Sanjay was debonair, tall and athletic. He was about thirty. He had joined the industry after his acting course from Pune Film Institute. He had acted in three Bhojpuri and two Hindi films already. His films had an average draw and he was trying for a big break to come up in the league of well-known actors. He had an apartment in Bandra where he lived with his wife and two children.

Ranbir wanted to try a known actor. Secondly, the role required a sensitive person. On both these counts, Sanjay had footed the bill.

Sanjay and Ranbir met at Flora and got themselves a middle table. In a few moments, the manager handed them the menu cards.

Ranbir asked, "Would you like some beer?"

Sanjay replied, "Yes, I would prefer draught beer."

"Would you like chicken spring rolls to go with it?"

"That is fine."

The manager took down the order, bowed courteously and went back.

Sanjay initiated the discussion, "I liked the script of *Aandhiyan*, and the film will appeal to the masses."

Ranbir nodded in agreement and added, "You and Meera are well suited for the roles."

They were served the beer, Kimchi salad and chicken spring rolls by a steward.

Ranbir asked, "You would be displaying multiple emotions like love, hatred and repentance in the role. Do you want to make some suggestions that could better the movie?"

Sanjay paused for a few moments and then spoke, "We should have an outdoor shoot for the love song. The background sound of something like a water fall would enhance the effect. We could go to Khandala, where there are excellent outdoor scenic places. "

"How about Punjabi poetry, especially where you remember your beloved and sing in her praise?" Ranbir asked.

"Yes poetry like, *Tere bin sanu sohnia koi hor nahio labhna.*" Sanjay hummed Rabbi Shergill's lyrics.

Ranbir consulted Sanjay about his preference for lunch. Then he glanced towards the steward and signalled him to come and take the order.

Both of them enjoyed the authentic Chinese food. Ranbir knew that Sanjay was smart and he would play his role well. The main purpose of the meeting was to get closer to him. They both needed each other to succeed.

15

Ranbir didn't have the background or academic qualifications in the field of human resources, but his attempt at making his first film taught him the importance of human relations. The success of a film depended on team work. He believed that each member of the team wanted to work in a healthy environment. He knew that being the producer and the director of the film it was his prime responsibility to keep his team motivated. He believed that better savings in film production could be achieved by producing and releasing the film in a record time rather than by squeezing the salaries of the team members. In addition to decent salaries, he provided them with free meals and tea during the shoots. He paid allowances towards their local transportations and also insured his team against accidents during the period of film production. In a short time, his team members got committed to their jobs and the pace of work increased.

He thought about his film from various angles to avoid any lacunas. He also hired an advertising agency for the promotion of his film.

In the first six months, they had completed the raw film. He had already recovered his dues of four crores from his debtors. He had also paid his team their dues and he was left with six crores towards Karkhanis's loan and some surplus. He had yet to sell his film and he had yet to spend on final dubbing, editing, advertising and promotion.

He organized a preview in a small theatre of about thirty seats at Colaba Causeway.

The film, before final dubbing and editing, was shown to the distributors, financers and the advertising company.

Aandhiyan *was a story of a young girl whose mother had passed away while giving birth. When she was still a child, father remarried. Her stepmother took care of her well materially, but she did not show much love towards her. She grew up in an atmosphere where she had a comfortable lifestyle, yet she yearned for love. She was very sensitive and expressed her love by appreciating nature. She loved flowers, rain drops, chirping birds, the changing seasons and colourful landscapes. She did well academically too.*

She grew up to be a beautiful woman. She joined a college in a city to do her graduation. She left her family and stayed in the girls' hostel there. She received the tragic news that her parents had passed away in a car accident. She went to her town to complete the last rites of her parents. During her stay there, she met a young man and they fell in love. He promised to marry her but deceived her and made good with all her valuables.

She sold all her inheritance, collected a moderate sum and moved to the city. She pursued her studies and stayed in the girls' hostel. She was heartbroken and financially strained and took the first job which came her way. Her employer was flirtatious; so to escape from his designs, she quit the job. She made efforts to improve her prospects, but failed repeatedly.

In her struggle she met another young man who brought happiness in her life. She considered him to be understanding, caring and soon she entered in a live-in relationship with him She was gullible and she thought that probably he wanted his younger sister to get settled first, before he proposed to her for marriage. To her shock, later she learnt that he was already married and he had a wife and two children in his hometown. She ended her illegitimate relationship acrimoniously and moved to another place.

She realized that she had had too many bad encounters. It seemed to be her fate. She finally committed suicide.

First the distributors' reactions were uncertain. Suleiman bhai from Delhi opened the discussion. He said that the film was good and its tragic end was serendipitous. He said that the film would be appreciated by the aam aadmi in north as well as east; the territories which he controlled.

Karim Sheikh spoke on behalf of the Mumbai territory. He said that the storyline was a bit weak. He said that the songs and outdoor scenic photography were the only highlights of the film, excepting which the film was barely average.

Their discussions went on for an hour; finally all the distributors and exporters were convinced by Suleiman's views. The story was alright and the scenic photography gave a special aura to the film.

Some of the shots in Khandala were breathtaking. The film had touching music and they unanimously accepted that public would enjoy it. They were reminded of the music of *Baiju Bawara* and *Anarkali* of the bygone era.

Karkhanis approached Ranbir and said, "Would you be interested in selling fifty percent of rights against my balance loan amount of five crores to you. Of course the balance expenses towards finishing, advertising and distribution would still be borne by you."

Ranbir was very happy to receive the offer.

He had learnt to bargain with Karkhanis in the past. He made a counter offer that against his loan, he could offer him thirty percent rights. He thought that he would be relieved of his liability of paying him his five crores and he would still own seventy percent rights of the film. Karkhanis accepted his counter offer.

The film required dubbing, editing and final processing. The dubbing was completed by Meera, Sanjay and other artists. That carried on for a month, and then the editor Ehsaan Husain and Ranbir got down to final editing and processing. They spent fifteen days in Cinemax Lab right from morning till evening. Finally the film was ready to be released.

The distributors decided to launch the film in all the territories, TV channels and overseas on the same date. They also decided to release the videos of the film after fifteen days of the launch. He got an advance of ten crores from the distributors. He paid three crores to Karkhanis, all his balance dues and also three crores towards advertising and publicity.

The banners had been put up at various strategic locations. Two of the film songs were being aired regularly on most of the FM channels in five metropolitan cities and twenty tier two cities across the country. On the day of the national release of the film, Ranbir was interviewed by a Zee Cinema and Radio Mirchi.

The film was successful from the word go. The analysts summarized the creative approach as the main reason for the success. The reviews were good and the two songs topped the charts for over two months. The film lifted Meera's star rating and Ranbir got recognition as the top director of the genre.

Ranbir made a clean profit of ten crores, which brought a measurable change in his lifestyle. He bought a three bedroom apartment in Versova and got it tastefully furnished. He also replaced his Ambassador by a Mercedes-Benz M Class.

16

Meera knew that to maintain a good figure, regular physical exercise was necessary. She made it a routine to jog for five kilometres on Palm Beach road and then do aerobics for fifteen minutes at home every morning. On the down side, she regretted her weakness for binging on non-vegetarian dishes and desserts.

She chose to spend more time with Sunanda to counter her weakness. She consulted her for diet recommendations. They often discussed what food should be eaten, how it should be cooked, what portions should be taken and what should be the suitable meal timings.

Sunanda was not so rigid about the diet because she knew that some concessions had to be made so that Meera could also enjoy the social get-togethers and functions. She knew that if the recommendations for the diet were too strict, then they would not be adhered to.

Meera's rule was that if she binged on food, then the next day she would burn out the extra calories in workouts. The rule translated into extra one kilometre jog and extra fifteen minutes of aerobics.

She enjoyed jogging for one more reason. She had made a few friends while jogging and she enjoyed their company.

The success of *Aandhiyan* had brought a sea change in her fortunes. She had appointed two IT geeks who projected her in social media. She had opened her Twitter and Facebook accounts. On certain days she had over ten thousand followers on Twitter. She had over two lakh friends on Facebook.

She had gained tremendous popularity and as a consequence, she had signed two more films and had got several modelling assignments. Wherever she went, she was cheered by crowds. Initially for almost a month, she suspected that her popularity was temporary, but when it remained steady with the passage of time, she was convinced that her fame would last long.

Chapter - II

1

Ranbir had signed Meera for his magnum opus production, *Payal Ki Jhankar*. She was offered two crores and the film budget had shot up to thirty-five crores.

He had been away for the workshop on film making and site seeing in US for a few weeks, and on his return he got busy with the production of the new film. He didn't realize that his over commitment to work would have a direct toll on his love affair with Meera.

Meera's success had made her nature amorphous. She couldn't hold on to the traditional concept of love.

Gossip had linked Meera with Karan, scion of a successful industrial empire in textiles, airlines and shipping. Rumour had it that she was getting a lot of attention from him. They were spotted in some of the parties together.

Ranbir had just returned home after a day of meetings with distributors. He sat down and poured a shot of Absolut Vodka with orange and switched on the TV. An anchor was giving the account of happenings in Bollywood, "We have the footage of the new love birds, Meera and Karan at a page three party."

The video showed Meera and Karan standing side by side leaning over the wall holding their drinks and chatting. There were over fifteen men and women enjoying the party around them. Meera was wearing a black sari and a sleeveless low cut blouse. She was smiling and looking into Karan's eyes.

Karan was wearing white trousers, white shoes and an orange shirt with large prints. He had hair up to his shoulders and he wore a gold chain around his neck. They seemed to be having a lively conversation.

Ranbir was stung with jealousy for the first time. He had never been bothered about the rumours and had considered rumours to be the superfluous baggage of celebrities. But in the video, he could see genuine interest in her eyes. He could also gauge in her an affinity towards the rich scion.

Ranbir finished his drink and switched the TV off. He was thinking deeply about his relationship with Meera in the recent past. He realized that during the last three months they had met only once, that too when he had signed her for his magnum opus and paid her. He was so deeply engaged in his work that his romantic involvement with her had taken a backseat. He had not expected a change in her and therefore he felt let down. He regretted that he took his intimacy with her for granted, while a flamboyant swashbuckler swooped down and stole her.

He went for a shower and changed into a kurta-pyjama. He made some vegetable sandwiches and had them for dinner. All through the night he tossed and turned, unable to get a wink of sleep. Only in early hours at dawn could he rest a little. When he woke up it was eight, and he had a bad headache. He pulled himself out of bed, popped two painkillers and went for a shower. He had an appointment with Ravi, the music director in Film City at eleven.

Ravi was in his late sixties. He had composed popular music in seventies. His music was soft and lyrical unlike the current music which was loud. His songs in *Aandhiyan* had revived public interest in romanticism. The box office success of the film had once again brought Ravi among the top music directors of Bollywood. He had credited Ranbir directly for his popularity because he was responsible for making a romantic film, when the trend was set for making action films.

Ranbir was feeling better by the time he reached Film City. He didn't have to wait long for Ravi. Ranbir was always punctual but Ravi had reached in time to show that he respected him as he was mostly late for appointments. In the past to the ire of a few, if Ravi anticipated that his to be acquaintances would not appreciate his music, he'd cancel the meetings at the last minute.

Ranbir was unhappy due to the distance which had come between him and Meera. He was not in a position to put his finger to what had led to the situation, but he was aware that the gap was palpable. He realized that during the last three months she had not invited him over even once. In the past, she would call him frequently and once in a while she would invite him for meals.

Ranbir thought of sharing his problem with Ravi because he was a mature and sensitive person. He gathered courage to finally ask him.

"Ravi ji, you give such lovely music to words, I am sure you are a romantic person?"

"Yes I am! Why do you ask?"

"I want some advice. Please keep it to yourself."

"Rest assured I will not say anything to anyone."

"I love Meera and she was also attracted towards me in the past. She had been overly nice to me. We met in Delhi when we were students in Delhi University. We met again in Mumbai when she was became a star. Then she became the heroine of my films. She even invited me for meals at her home a number of times and she often cooked for me. We kissed each other; I offered her bouquets of flowers which she accepted lovingly. She even offered me two crores as a loan when I was in financial difficulties, though I didn't take it. I thought that I would propose to her after I achieve success. To my dismay, now when I've done pretty well for myself, instead of getting closer we have drifted apart. We hardly meet each other apart from work related meetings. Last night I saw her on TV, partying with Karan, the industrialist. She seemed to be very close to him and the media is talking about their affair."

Ravi listened to him patiently and then he answered with cynicism, "That is the nature of a beautiful woman. You cannot expect loyalty from her. She is like a butterfly, who keeps displaying her colours to many wooers."

Ranbir said, "Don't you think you are being unfair in painting all beautiful women with the same brush? I am heartbroken!"

"I would suggest that you forget about Meera and find a dependable woman. She is a film star; she will only bring pain. You deal with her only professionally. Once your present film *Payal Ki Jhankar* is completed, then choose a new heroine. You should also get married to a simple girl."

Ranbir let out a mirthless laugh and commented, "You have given me worldly advice. Have you been so practical in your personal life also?"

"I had been a fool in my younger days. That is why I lived a miserable life."

"I thought you had been quite successful as a music director."

"I was very creative and successful when I came to the film industry in the mid sixties. I got recognition and money. Then I got sentimental about a woman who didn't care about my feelings. I neglected my work and spent a great fortune on her. To my shock, she left me for one of my close friends. I remained heartbroken and depressed, and as a result, for thirty-five years I couldn't achieve anything. I lived on the fringes. Finally success came to me only in the last five years. But how does it matter now? I have already lived most of my life."

Ranbir thought that it had been worthwhile to take Ravi's advice. After all, he was much senior to him in age as well as profession.

"Thanks very much for your advice and I shall try to follow it."

They spent the rest of the time composing and discussing the music for the film. They were absorbed in work for about two hours, to finally part at eight o'clock.

Ranbir dropped in at Anandya, a newly-opened spa at Inorbit Mall, Goregaon. He was greeted by the receptionist and he was requested to wait. The interiors were tastefully designed. The receptionist provided him with a catalogue and asked him to select one among various kinds of therapeutic massages available. He chose to go for a Balinese full body massage.

A young masseuse in her mid-twenties escorted him to a small room. The room was dimly lit with a few candles and was decorated with a flower vase. It had wooden interiors and a pleasant aroma. There was a long pedestal table covered with a white sheet. He was requested to change and lie down.

His mind was obsessed with Meera's thoughts and his body was exhausted due to lack of sleep and over work. He had the feeling of guilt when he was at the spa.

The masseuse washed his feet with warm water and she gave him a nice olive oil massage from head to toe for an hour.

She asked him to take a bath in an adjoining shower room. His body felt rejuvenated after the massage and the shower. She offered him hot jasmine tea with cashew nuts and almonds after the therapy.

Ranbir reached home, still obsessed with thoughts about Meera. The news and the video about Meera and Karan's love affair were vividly sketched in his memory. He felt a sharp pain in his guts; his mind was obsessed with Meera's desertion. He was unable to come to terms with the changed situation.

He thought of sharing his problem with Meera's cousin, Sunanda. He called her up on her mobile.

"Hello Ranbir, it is a pleasant surprise to receive your call after our last meeting at Meera's house."

He said with a heavy heart, "I had been occupied with work. My second film released recently and now I am in the process of making my third film. Your suggestions on advertising and promotion were very useful and my second film was a box office success. I am thankful to you."

"I am glad to know that. But why are you sounding so low?"

"Can we meet today?"

"Okay, my shift will be over at six in the evening. If you like we can meet at New Yorker at Chowpatty at 6.30."

"I will be there, thanks very much."

At New Yorker, Ranbir occupied a table near the window from where he could watch the road. In about five minutes Sunanda entered the restaurant. She smiled at him and sat opposite him.

"Hey, it has been over a year since we met. You have become slimmer," she said with a smile.

"You look very pretty and your glasses make you look like a doctor," he responded.

She gave an angelic smile and enquired, "Thanks, now what made you remember me?"

"I got so involved with my work that I did not realize that my personal relationship also needed nurturing." He poured out his heart.

"You mean your relationship with Meera?"

"Yes, though we meet professionally, we have distanced ourselves in our personal lives."

"It is strange. You could loosen up a little and have a chat with her."

"I doubt whether it would help."

"I think you should leave it to fate," she added empathetically after some thought.

"I am simply crestfallen and I have lost the zest for life. I was looking forward to spending my life with her. My inspiration has gone." He spoke remorsefully.

Sunanda put her hand on Ranbir's hand and pressed it lightly. She said considerately, "Don't lose heart, things will be alright."

Sunanda was a compassionate woman. She realized that he was very hurt.

"I shall try to find out what is going on." She assured him.

He had a glimmer of hope and he thought that there may be a chance that Meera still loved him. He decided not to jump to conclusions, though.

"Thanks very much, I will wait to hear from you."

2

Karan and Meera stood on the deck holding their champagne glasses. It was a starry night and all around them they could see the dark expanse of sea. The Star Cruiser reverberated with the beats of a popular song.

Karan wore dark denim trousers, a white shirt, and a black corduroy coat. Meera was draped in a golden gown. Karan had invited twenty guests on board his private Star Cruiser for the party. He had met Meera in one of the parties after the success of *Aandhiyan*. She also liked his effable nature and therefore when he invited her to his Star Cruiser, she accepted his proposal.

"I hope you are enjoying yourself?" Karan asked gallantly.

"Oh, it is wonderful!" Meera replied with an engaging smile.

"When I come here on the deck under the sky and see the vast ocean around, I forget all my worries."

"I love to be surrounded by nature as well. My apartment has a clear view of the ocean."

Karan moved closer to Meera and put his hand on her shoulder. The ship was smoothly sailing away from the shimmering lights of Queen's Necklace. The cool breeze was blowing on their faces. Karan brought his face close to Meera's and lightly kissed her on the lips. She liked the feeling, but withdrew herself.

Karan by habit didn't fancy the slow game of coveting a young woman, yet he treaded cautiously this time as the woman in question was beautiful and a successful film star. He was young, bashful and cocky. He was content that she had accepted his invitation and she had liked his overtures. This in itself assured him that it was a successful beginning.

"Have you visited the exhibition of Anjolie Ela Menon's paintings at Chemould Gallery which is on these days?" Karan used his charm to impress her. His family was known for their art collection.

Meera was extra deferential to Karan, the scion of a successful industrial empire. She wanted further meetings so replied with enthusiasm, "No, I have not, but it would be a treat to see her paintings!"

"If you like, we can have lunch at the Taj tomorrow and after that we can go see the paintings."

Meera thought about her schedule. She had a modelling shoot at five at Malabar Hills.

"If I can reach Malabar Hills by four, then I can go with you." She politely mentioned her constraints.

"Meet me at the Taj at twelve tomorrow. We will be free by 3.30."

"Fine, I'll see you there."

The party got livelier with the music being played.

Karan held Meera's hand and invited her to the dance floor. She walked with him and they danced together. A number of songs were played for over half an hour, while a few more couples joined in.

Finally Karan and Meera walked back to the deck. Dinner was ready and was being served on the lower deck.

The party continued till midnight. The Star Cruiser finally dropped them at Lion Gate at Ballard Pier. Karan came up to Meera's new 3.0 TDI Audi car to bid her goodnight. They waved good night to each other.

3

Meera had seen her name being associated with Karan in film magazines, TV channels and on page three of the dailies. Initially she was concerned about the gossip as it was influencing her relationship with Ranbir. Before the launch of *Aandhiyan,* she had been sentimentally attached with him, but some changes had occurred in their relationship in the last six months. She had been over the moon after the success of the film. Finally her busy schedule and a bigger launch of her fourth film had taken the final toll on their love life. She had been showered with invitations, offers for modelling assignments and sponsorships. She had made one crore from *Aandhiyan*, two crores from modelling, one crore from sponsorships, and another two crores as advance for *Payal Ki Jhankar*. Her market value had zoomed and she had signed another film for three crores under Pooja Bhatt's banner. She had not imagined that Karan, a billionaire industrialist would be her suitor. He had dashing looks and was charming. Though he had a public image of a casanova, she wanted to give him the benefit of doubt. She didn't want to give any credence to hearsay comments.

She was a little concerned about the effect of the gossip on Ranbir. She thought that he was mature enough to understand the changed circumstances. She was being catapulted as a successful diva partially due to her closeness to Karan. She decided to go with the current without being too bothered about Ranbir's sentiments. However, her associates – including her mother – did not approve of her affair with Karan.

4

Meera's phone rang. It was Sunanda on the line.

"Hey, are you very busy?" Sunanda checked up.

"Oh no, I have my shoot at seven in the evening. I am free till five; are you coming over?" Meera inquired happily.

"I will reach your place by twelve. Wanted to spend some time together."

"I will ask the maid to make your favourite mutton curry and potato capsicum."

"Cool. I will get rasgullas from Tiwari Sweets."

It was Sunanda's day off.

Meera and Sunanda hugged each other when they met. They sat in the drawing room sipping tea and got down to narrating their latest experiences.

"I have heard that you and Karan have developed a special liking towards each other," Sunanda broached the topic casually.

"How did you know that?" Meera asked with a playful smile.

"I saw it on TV. A clip of you guys together at a party!"

"Oh yes, Karan is a dude."

"Do you truly fancy him or is it just flirting?"

"Presently, I can say that I like him, but I don't know, in the future our friendship could develop into something special."

"But Karan has an image of a playboy." Sunanda tried to dissuade her.

"It is hearsay. People are jealous of his good fortune," Meera shot back. She looked hurt.

"What about Ranbir? I thought you liked him?" Sunanda was careful.

"Yes I did, but he does not value my feelings. I waited for him."

"Maybe he wanted to be successful before proposing to you?"

"Probably yes, but I could not go on acting under his direction, subjugating all my feelings. I was lonely and miserable. Fortunately I met Karan and he brought sunshine into my life."

"Is there a possibility of your going back to Ranbir?"

"No, I am happy with Karan."

Sunanda realized that Meera's success had gone to her head. She was a diva and she was being courted by a successful tycoon. The odds seemed stacked against Ranbir.

Meera did not guess that Sunanda had spoken to her being Ranbir's emissary.

Sunanda decided not to probe any further and changed the subject. Lunch was served and they relished the sumptuous meal.

After lunch, they shifted to the drawing room and continued the banter. They were interrupted at four by the maid, who had brought coffee and cookies for them.

Soon after, Sunanda left Meera's house. She reached home and called up Ranbir.

"I met Meera for lunch today. I broached the subject of her feelings towards you. She mentioned that you didn't pay any attention to her and that she felt very lonely. In the meantime, she met Karan, who cared for her and then she began dating him. She wants to carry on with you only professionally," Sunanda clarified, trying to be as gentle as possible.

Ranbir heard Sunanda and he felt depressed when she confirmed Meera's change of heart. He thanked Sunanda for her help.

"Ranbir, don't take it to heart!" Sunanda gave him friendly advice.

When she didn't hear his reply, she knew that the news had hit Ranbir hard. She felt very concerned about him and suggested, "If you like, we can meet at Mainland China at Lokhandwala and have dinner together."

"Okay, let's meet at nine."

5

Ranbir felt forlorn and low; he was unable to forget Meera.

Sunanda tried to cheer him up, "Hey don't look so glum!"

Ranbir tried to smile and walked with her to a side table.

They ordered a bottle of Anakena, a Chilean white wine.

Sunanda moved her hand slowly and placed it over his hand.

"Cheer up!" she tried engaging him in a conversation.

"I am feeling really low after learning about Meera's change of heart. I don't know how I'll complete my present film. Whenever I see Karan with Meera I feel as if I have been stabbed in the heart and that he is twisting the blade. My pain gets unbearable." He shared his trauma.

She felt very compassionate and remained quiet for a few moments.

"I have a suggestion. You may follow it if you consider it worthwhile."

"Say!" He looked at her hopefully.

"You can probably channelize your emotions which you have towards Meera into directing your film." Sunanda suggested as a well wisher.

He thought over her words.

"Life is a journey, one has to complete it!" He lamented.

She was not of much help in lifting his spirits.

They ordered their meal and munched their food slowly. They spent most of the evening sitting and musing quietly. She knew that his wound was raw and it would heal only with time.

Finally he called the waiter for the bill.

"It is my treat." She moved her hand towards her purse.

"It doesn't matter, you can pay the next time." He suggested and paid the bill with a tip.

They walked out to the front. In a few moments, her driver and the restaurant valet brought their cars. They both bade each other goodbye and then left for their homes.

6

Meera and Karan flew to Nice, a city of southeast France on the Mediterranean Sea northeast of Cannes. Controlled by various royal houses after the 13th century, the city was finally ceded to France in 1860. It is the leading resort city of the French Riviera.

A short drive from the airport and they were in the beautiful locales at the picturesque resort town Cannes, where the film festival was on. Meera had been invited as a successful diva from Bollywood. She wore a light green gown designed by Vallya, and complimented it with white stilettos. Her tresses were in soft curls which fell over her bare shoulder. She looked radiant when she walked on the red carpet with film celebrities from different countries.

Karan and Meera were to stay in Hotel Martinez on the beach. Meera was very happy as she seemed to have accomplished all that a young woman could dream of. She was a celebrity and she had money. She was soon to get married to a successful industrialist icon. She had not even imagined that within a few years she would be able to achieve so much.

Karan played a song on his phone.

Meera came into Karan's arms; they kissed passionately and lowered themselves on the bed. Meera opened his shirt buttons and kissed his bare chest. Karan opened her gown and then freed her voluptuous breasts, pressing them with his mouth. Meera was feeling ecstatic, she unzipped Karan's trousers and moved her hand inside and held his manhood, which by her sheer touch grew bigger and became erect.

They clung to each other totally naked and made love with frenzy. They lay together fully satiated. They were in full mood to celebrate every moment of their togetherness. They later changed and drank Glenlivet single malt scotch with ice and potatoes chips.

In the next few days, they toured Nice, Monaco, Monte Carlo, and Cannes. These places were very picturesque. Karan also gifted a sapphire and pearl necklace to Meera at St. Paul.

7

The dance was being choreographed at the film city. Meera was playing a courtesan in *Payal Ki Jhankar*. The shooting was to cover solo dance in a palace. The choreographer Saroj, music director Ravi, cameraman Fali Mistry along with Ranbir and the technical team were on the set. The dance steps were based on Kathak.

It was the third take of the same shot in which Meera had to take three full circles and then come to a still pose where she looked like a statue from Ajanta caves. She looked beautiful in her attire and make-up as a courtesan, but in each shot she was getting unsteady during the third turn and the shot had to be repeated.

Everyone on the set was getting impatient, except Ranbir. He realized that she did not seem to be as serious towards her work as she had been in the past. She had two films on floor, seven modelling and sponsorship assignments on and she had been on a holiday to Monte Carlo and Cannes with Karan during the last seven days. Ranbir had evolved a very healthy work culture on his sets. All those who had worked with him were fully aware that each and every artist, technician and even extras were treated with full respect. No one was ever admonished there. That was the reason that every team member gave his or her best contribution.

Ranbir handled the situation patiently. He gave a cue to Saroj and she announced a tea break for everyone.

Meera looked a little peevish when she walked towards the choreographer, music director and Ranbir.

"I am sorry. I don't know why I am faltering each time." She said.

"I know you'll do it. Just calm down and try," Saroj recommended politely.

Meera looked apologetic as she knew that she was at fault. There was a perceptible tension in the air.

Ranbir thought, "The shoot will have to be postponed for some other day, when she is ready after adequate practice. That means that the day's investment of five lakhs and the time of five senior persons and the technical team will go waste. My interest burden is also growing at a rate of fifty thousand every day."

While tea was being served, Karan in his flamboyant style walked on to the set. He straight went to Meera and held her hand.

Meera looked pleasantly surprised and her mood changed for the better. Ranbir had not seen Karan face to face till then. He had seen him only on television and in magazines. He felt a stab of jealousy when he saw Meera and Karan holding each other's hands, smiling and talking. Other members of the team were also surprised to see the tycoon walking on to the set totally unannounced.

Ravi, the music director, was the first one to discreetly disapprove Karan's unannounced visit *on the set.*

"Ranbir, I don't think with all these distractions she will be able to devote much attention to her role."

Saroj also looked serious. She looked at her watch and said, "Ranbir, please, I have to leave now. We are done for the day."

The shooting was called off for the day.

Ranbir and Ravi were the only two persons who remained on the set after the rest of the members had left.

Ravi commented, "You have invested too much on her. After *Aandhiyan,* you should have chosen a different heroine."

Ranbir looked distraught when he sadly mentioned, "This glamour world is like a bubble. It grows bigger and bigger and then bursts all of a sudden!"

"The situation is not as grim as you have painted it. Meera and you are professionals. You can still complete the film. You should just remember to not allow your emotions to take control over you."

Ranbir understood Ravi's advice, but he also felt helpless in having to work with her.

"Thanks very much, I will try to be as professional as possible," he replied respectfully.

They walked to the parking lot and parted ways.

As Ranbir walked towards his car, he thought about what Sunanda and Ravi had said. She had advised him that he should channelize his love for Meera into making his film as a work of art. Ravi had recommended that he should act professionally without his feelings of hurt or betrayal interfering with his work.

He sat on the driving seat of his Mercedes-Benz and switched on the ignition, the air conditioning and slowly steered the car out of Film City.

He knew that Sunanda would be busy in the operation theatre in the hospital. He didn't have any more intimate friends. The next two days were off due to the weekend. He finally decided to go and watch *The Curious Case of Benjamin Button* which had received many Oscar nominations.

8

Ranbir's film *Payal Ki Jhankar* was a magnum opus. He did a mental calculation of his accounts. He had fixed a budget of thirty-five crores for the film. He had put in ten crores of his own money in it. His distributors had invested another fifteen crores. He had borrowed five crores from Karkhanis. He had planned to borrow five crores more for publicity about a month before the release.

This time everything chosen was the best.

The sets were very expensive. Two locales in New Zealand were chosen after proper research. He had booked a dance shoot in Rambagh Palace in Jaipur. The dresses were designed by renowned designer, Sunit Verma and Meera's vintage ornaments were designed by Kisna jewellers.

He wondered whether his changed relationship with Meera would have a bearing on his film. He shuddered at the thought of her dropping out of the film or delaying the film. He was worried because he had not signed any detailed agreement with her.

He thought pessimistically, "She is the central character of my film. If she doesn't give her best, the film will suffer."

His worries caused palpitations in his body. That was the first time that he felt physical discomfort. He was perspiring and was feeling numbness in his left arm. He got alarmed and he pressed Sunanda's number on his mobile.

"Hello, I am a little unwell and I am having some palpitations and numbness in my left arm. Can you please come over to my place?

"Oh sure, don't worry, just loosen your clothes and lie down in an airy place. What's your address?" She replied reassuringly.

He sent her his address in a message and tried to be calm.

She got the SMS and called him back, "I will be at your place within an hour."

She arrived in an hour and checked his condition. They slowly walked to her car. She asked the driver to take them to Kokilaben Hospital. He got his blood pressure and electro cardiogram taken there.

Ranbir's blood pressure was high and his cardiogram showed some abnormality. The doctor gave him some medicines and prescribed rest for three days. Ranbir thanked Sunanda for her help. She smiled warmly. She dropped him home to take rest and then left for the hospital.

The rest rejuvenated him. He also realized that he should stop worrying. Later Sunanda fixed his appointment with a well-known cardiologist, Dr Nariman.

Sunanda accompanied him to the clinic.

Dr Nariman commented, "I normally do not examine anyone who is below thirty! However, as you are already here, you may lie down."

He examined him thoroughly.

Dr Nariman finally briefed him, "You are absolutely fit. Your TMT can be helpful after twenty years for a comparison. Do you smoke?"

"Thank you. I am a casual smoker."

"Give up smoking. You are absolutely fine. You may go now."

Ranbir felt as light as a bird. He happily walked out to meet Sunanda and informed her about Dr Nariman's diagnosis. She was also relieved to know that he was fine.

The weather was very pleasant and he drove his car to Chowpatty. He parked his car there and walked on the wet sand along the sea. He was relaxed and happy.

In the last four days, he had not thought about his film. He had stopped thinking about Meera as well. He had understood that his health was top priority. He realized that he had undertaken a major responsibility of completing a magnum opus and that he could not afford to be unhealthy!

He stopped at a newly-opened gym near his apartment. He walked in to see the facilities. He enrolled himself and paid registration charges and six months' fees in advance. He was happy with his decision.

The first few days of shooting with Meera were very painful. He would often find her scribbling Karan's name on rough pads or texting messages or calling him. The other members of the unit would often discuss her boyfriend and in response she would blush and become extra playful. She would also tell them about her dates with him. She also told them about their forthcoming trip to Khandala.

Ranbir felt hurt but he had to be strong so that he wouldn't be affected. He thought that he was the director of a love story and his being more sensitive than others could in a way enhance the quality of his film. He also realized his mistake. He had been unable to understand her strong need for love when she was romantically involved with him. He should have been more demonstrative at that time and he should have expressed his love to her openly. He should have in fact told her that he wanted to marry her and he should have discussed his plans with her. Alas, that was not to be!

9

Karan had organized a meeting between Meera and his parents at their bungalow in Juhu. Meera was fidgety as she looked anxiously at Karan. His parents were due to arrive from the airport at any moment.

"Karan, do you love me?" Meera asked him to reassure herself.

Karan was also tense. He mumbled, "Of course I do!"

Karan called for the servant and asked Meera if she wanted something.

"I need a glass of water," she answered nervously.

There was a sound of a horn outside the gate. They heard the security guards opening the main gate. The black Mercedes-Benz

SL Class came into the porch. A guard opened the rear door and Karan's parents alighted from the backseat and walked inside the hall.

When they entered, both Karan and Meera got up from their seats. Karan walked up to his parents and introduced Meera to them.

Meera smiled and greeted them respectfully.

Karan's parents looked pompous and Karan's mother responded condescendingly, "Good morning Meera, we have seen your films. You are a good actor."

"Thanks, Karan often talks about you." Meera responded deferentially to get their acceptance.

Karan's father also nodded and gestured to her to sit down as they sank into the armed sofa chairs.

"We are going to have tea, would you like to have some too?" Karan's mother checked with Meera.

"Sure Aunty, may I have green tea?"

"Good, you must be disciplined about your diet."

Meera preened towards Karan and smiled for support.

Karan tried to dissipate the tension in the air, "We have been having junk food. She had golgappas last evening."

Karan's mother smiled. She said, "Unfortunately, I had not been able to spend much time with Karan during his growing years. That is why he has become quite spoilt. We hope you would be able to control his wild nature!"

Both Karan and Meera laughed.

Meera realized that Karan's father still looked serious. He had not joined the banter. He made a serious point, "We understand that you are planning to get married. How would you support Karan to take our industrial empire to a higher level?"

Meera got serious after hearing the question.

"I will support him in his business."

"How? You are an actor. Would you give up your career?"

"I can't do that immediately as I have signed two films, which are on the floor. I will not sign any new film."

"When would these two films be ready?"

"In two years."

"I think the producers of your films at the time of release, after two years, would not like it if the heroine of their films gets married. I'm sure you'd have to wait for another year to get married. Do you think that our business empire can wait that long for such a crucial decision?"

"Papa, that is my part. I will be working towards expanding our business, irrespective of whether I am married or not," Karan mentioned.

The tea and snacks had been laid out on the table.

Karan's father received a business call and he excused himself. Karan had switched on light music in the background and once again the atmosphere lightened up.

10

Ranbir was hard at work trying to complete the movie and Meera was also giving her best performance. The film was supposed to have a happy ending but before that, Meera dropped a bombshell. One day he learnt from one of his unit members that she was crying. She had come to the set after her break up with Karan. She looked thin and her eyes looked sunken with dark shadows underneath. She looked heartbroken.

He heard it through the grapevine that Karan's father had not approved of Meera. Karan would have inherited nothing if he went against his Dad's wishes. They had already zeroed on to an industrialist's daughter and Karan had given his consent to marry her.

The shooting was called off. When Ranbir reached home, he realized that it had been about one year since Meera had been head over heels in love with Karan. He switched on the TV and changed the channels. On Zee, he saw Koyal airing her show about Bollywood news. She announced the breaking news that Meera, the successful film actress and Karan, the successful industrialist had broken off their year-long love affair. She said that Meera would even get her tattoo with the initial 'K' removed from the nape of her neck.

Ranbir felt sorry for her. He realized she would need a reassuring voice at this time. He picked up his phone and bolstered his courage to dial her number. He found that her phone was engaged. He waited for ten minutes and dialled her number once again. After a few rings, he heard her voice.

"Hello Ranbir," she spoke in a low voice.

"Hello Meera, we haven't met for a long time. Would you like to go out for dinner tonight?"

"Okay! How about meeting at The Leela at eight?"

He felt cheerful and disconnected the line after agreeing to her suggestion.

Ranbir called her and told her to occupy a table at The Great Wall restaurant at The Leela and order something. He said that he would be with her in ten minutes.

When he walked up to her table. he was wondering whether she was the same girl whom he was so madly in love with. Meera wore a light blue t-shirt with a pair of jeans. She looked pale without any makeup on her face.

He nodded and sat opposite her. The next moment she was shedding tears. She was aghast to learn about Karan's change of heart. He had gone for an arranged match to satisfy his father's wishes. She was mourning his treachery.

"What would you like to have?" Ranbir asked politely to change her mood.

"Nothing. I am not hungry!" she replied sobbing.

"I can't sit here and eat alone! You should have something."

"Fine. A sweet corn soup."

"Vegetarian?"

"Yes!"

He ordered two vegetarian soups and then looked at her.

"Please cheer up."

She took out two tissues from her purse and dried her tears.

She even tried to give a faint smile.

"Ranbir, thanks for your patience with me."

"I have decided to change the ending of the film. Instead of a happy ending, it will be a tragedy," he said.

"Why, are you serious?" she enquired.

"For a magnum opus, a tragic ending would be way more suitable! Look at *Mughal-e-Azam, Devdas, Umrao Jaan,* and the likes."

"Will Varun make the necessary changes in the script?

"After seeing you in the present state, it was his idea. He said he would change the script and show it to me within three days," Ranbir said.

"Are you drawing a parallel between my real life and my reel life?" Meera asked with a faint smile.

"No, I was thinking about how the film would be remembered in the future," he said seriously.

"It is ironical that in film-making, you can use my personal tragedy to make me look larger than life."

"Do you think I am being insensitive towards you?"

"As a film producer and the director of the film, you have larger commitment towards its success! Moreover, I also think it should have a tragic end."

"I will send you the revised script in three days and then if you like it, we can start shooting within a week. The film should get completed in the next three months."

11

Payal Ki Jhankar was launched with a lot of fanfare. The film received good critical reviews for its artistic performance and sensitive direction.

Meera's break up with Karan had affected her public image. She had lost the charisma of a fresh young girl. And within that time, a few newcomers had made their mark.

Payal Ki Jhankar did not draw crowds as *Aandhiyan* had done. It was a major blow to Meera's career. In a complete reversal, in a couple of months she had lost all the sponsorship campaigns. Her other film under Pooja Bhatt was shelved as well.

An actress's career in Bollywood is normally short because the public prefers younger heroines. Meera had spent about six years in the film industry already, and she no longer had the enigma of a fresh heroine. She had sent feelers to different producers for new roles, but hadn't got any positive response. Her broken affair had made her aloof and a lot more serious. She could not bring herself to request Ranbir to start a new film with her.

Ranbir had been through a lot of hardships. Luckily, he could keep his two main assets, home and the car intact. He didn't have the nerve to produce another film after the lack-lustre response to his magnum opus.

Ranbir had spent four years in Mumbai in the industry. He had gained a lot of experience in film making. He had three releases to his credit, including one box office hit. His financial position had peaks and troughs. However, on the quality front, the film veterans had credited him for producing artistic films. Only in his first film, *Aaj Ki Shaam* did he succumb to commercial pressures, such as introducing two item numbers with a lot of skin show. In his second and third films, he did not make any compromises. His second film *Aandhiyan* was liked by all and sundry and it catapulted him as well as his heroine Meera to new heights. The success also gave him the strength to produce the magnum opus *Payal Ki Jhankar*, a film which got him good reviews, though it could not draw the crowds. He lost over five crores in the film.

Chapter - III

1

Ranbir read the congratulatory letter twice. He had been awarded the best director of the year for his film *Payal Ki Jhankar* for excellence in cinematic achievements in Indian Cinema. He was feeling elated that he had been honoured with the prestigious National award. He was also invited to Vigyan Bhawan to receive it. The award would be presented by the President of India in a special function.

He shared the news with Meera.

"Hello, I have some good news to share. I have received the best director of the year title for our film by the Directorate of Film Festivals. I must say that it was due to the team effort that we could create a work of art. I would like you to join me at the function at Vigyan Bhawan in New Delhi."

She responded, "Congratulations for the award, but I am sorry, I will not be able to come as I will be busy with a modelling assignment."

Meera felt a pang of jealousy when she heard that he had received the best director award. She was wallowing in self pity for getting ignored by the film industry during the last three months. Only a year-and-a-half back she had been the cynosure of all the glitterati. She had the media hovering around her all the time and had been the darling of the masses. Ranbir had also loved her. Unfortunately, times had changed.

Ranbir was disappointed but he did not press her, "Okay thanks."

He made the next call to Sunanda and shared the good news with her.

She was extremely happy to receive the news. "Oh, it is wonderful. It is a great honour and I believe the President of India presents the award in a big ceremony at Vigyan Bhawan?"

He said happily, "Yes, I was so surprised to receive the news. I still can't believe it!"

"Did you share the news with Meera?"

"Yes, I did. I even invited her to accompany me to the function but she refused and said she was busy with a modelling assignment."

Sunanda could feel compassion in his voice.

"That doesn't matter. You must not let it dampen your happiness."

"Sunanda, it would be wonderful if you'd join me at the function."

She felt butterflies in her stomach. She was delighted to receive the invitation. She once thought about the effect of her accompanying Ranbir to the function on Meera. She knew Meera wouldn't like it. But she didn't let her feeling of guilt suppress her present happiness.

"Yes, it would be my pleasure."

Ranbir had some rest after the release of *Payal Ki Jhankar*. Earlier he had not dwelt on starting another film because of the difficulties he had undergone, but he got a lot of inspiration after receiving the news about the national award. He thought that he could make a woman-centric film with Meera as the heroine. He had made all his films with her and overall as a heroine she had proven to be lucky for him. Their screen chemistry as director and heroine was still going strong, even though their relationship had ended.

2

Ranbir's heart filled with pride as the car passed the black marble arch with the Asoka emblem – the entrance to Vigyan Bhawan. Along the way, the goblet-shaped street lights looked enchanting. Ranbir and Sunanda walked through the courtyard where the water fountain bubbling in the black enclosure created a feeling of tranquillity. On arriving at the east gate after the security check, they were escorted to Hall I on the second floor. The hall had a capacity for approximately two hundred and fifty people and was packed.

Ranbir and Sunanda were escorted to their seats in the second row of the auditorium. It was filled with awardees, invitees from the film industry, politicians, bureaucrats, well-known industrialists, VIPs and security staff. In the background, Bhim Sen Joshi's *thumri* reverberated.

In a few minutes, the President arrived accompanied by the Minister of Information and Broadcasting and his retinue of security personnel. They were guided to the front row. The President was respectfully seated in the middle. After a little while she was escorted to the stage to inaugurate the function by lighting the lamp and to address the invitees. Thereafter, the compere took over and commenced the show by announcing the name of the first recipient of the award. It was in the category of the best film for children. She gave the highlights of the film and the award went to Nandan Paritosh for best direction. He walked to the stage and the President handed him a gold medallion.

There were awards in the category of non feature films and feature films. Finally the award for the best direction in Hindi cinema category was announced. The compere gave a synopsis of *Payal Ki Jhankar* and then she mentioned a few words about Ranbir. She described him as a director of the romantic genre. Everyone was waiting to look at Ranbir because of the popularity of Hindi commercial cinema. Ranbir proudly walked to the stage and the President presented him the gold medallion.

The live telecast was on and lakhs of viewers were watching him receiving the honour. The ceremony was followed by a special dinner in the courtyard. There were beautifully laid out carts with traditional vegetarian food.

Ranbir and Sunanda were interrupted by an interviewer from Star TV. She asked, "Hello, I am Bhawana. It would be my pleasure if you allow me to ask you some questions for a live telecast."

Ranbir agreed and the next moment he and Sunanda were on the TV screen on the wall.

"You have been the producer and director for your film *Payal Ki Jhankar*. When you started making the film, what was on top of your mind? The quality of the film or your film being a box office hit?"

Ranbir smiled and reminisced before answering. "When I make a film, I always have to put in all my savings as well as borrow from whatever sources are available to me. Under such pressure, I am always hoping for my film to be a box office success. But I get motivated to make a quality film first and foremost."

Bhawana asked her next question, "Your films are invariably centred on a woman and Meera has always been the heroine of your films. Do you share a special bond with her?"

Ranbir said, "This is a personal question, I would prefer not to reply."

Bhawana smiled and said, "Would you like to say something about your next film?"

"It will be a woman-centric film."

"Will Meera be heroine of your next film?"

"I will prefer that, but I haven't asked her yet."

Bhawana thanked him. Some of the invitees had approached Ranbir for his autograph.

Sunanda was left alone, and as a result, was feeling self conscious. After Ranbir's interview, some of the invitees had started looking at her curiously.

Ranbir did not realize that Sunanda was jealous that despite his heartbreak, Meera remained the cynosure of his being, to the extent that he still wanted to cast her as the heroine. She wondered why she had accompanied him from Mumbai to Delhi. She felt self conscious that people around them and those who were watching the TV program knew that she was Ranbir's escort, but in his heart, he adored Meera.

She excused herself and left him busy talking to some of the guests. He could not ask her anything at that moment, though he could guess that something was amiss. In a few minutes he went outside to look for her. He called her up on her mobile, but it was switched off. He was informed by the reception committee that she had already left for the hotel. He requested the person in charge to arrange for a car to drop him to the hotel.

He called up Sunanda's room on the intercom after reaching the hotel lobby.

He heard her voice, "Hello!"

"Hello, Ranbir here. I am sorry if I have said something wrong. I know you are upset due to some reason. I want to come to your room and apologize."

"No, there is nothing. I had a headache so I came back to rest. Anyway, I am feeling better now and if you wish, you can come up to my room."

He thanked her and walked to the lift. Once the lift reached her floor, he walked to her door quickly. He knocked, pushed the door open and stepped inside. He saw her sitting on her bed with her feet up and her head on the back rest.

He closed the door and went and sat down next to her. For the first time he felt the excitement of sitting next to her in the privacy of a luxurious hotel. He looked up and saw tears in her eyes.

He couldn't help himself and cupped her face in his palms and asked, "What happened?"

She could not restrain her emotions and big tears rolled down her pink cheeks.

He pulled her head towards himself and held it to his chest. They sat motionless, quietly listening to each other's heartbeats for a few moments.

"Why are you crying on such a happy occasion?"

"I think I am in love with you. I felt jealous when you said that you wanted Meera to be the heroine of your next film in the interview."

He smiled and kissed her. She also kissed him back passionately. He realized that she was amorous and she held him tightly. The next moment he pressed his body against hers and he passionately kissed her mouth, cheeks, eyes and breasts. The arousal was spontaneous, and they rolled on the bed and slipped out of their clothes.

They felt ecstatic as they had not realized how much they had wanted each other. They made passionate love and satiated, they lay in each other's arms for some time. She didn't have to explain anything to him in words.

3

Ranbir was in a quagmire after making love to Sunanda. On one side he was proclaiming in public that Meera would be the heroine of his next film. In his heart he was still in love with her. On the other hand, he had just involved himself physically with Sunanda, who was Meera's best friend and cousin. He feared that it would have consequences and he would not be able to escape the fallout.

Ranbir and Sunanda were seated next to each other on their flight to Mumbai. She had been more caring towards him after their physical intimacy, even though she had not expressed anything about her expectations from him.

Ranbir had Meera on his mind; he hoped that she would understand his visit to Delhi with Sunanda. He hoped that she would return to him after her break up with Karan and she would regret her relationship with Karan. He dreamt that she was in love with him and they were together in Khandala.

He thought, "Will Sunanda forget about what happened between us in her room? Will she let go of the memory of our passionate love making?"

He looked at Sunanda as she slept with her head on his shoulder with a light smile on her face. She looked very charming. He could not deny the thrill he had experienced in her company. She had been able to fill in the void which had been created due to Meera's absence.

There was an announcement to fasten the seat belts and straighten up the seats as the plane was about to land. Sunanda woke up from her sleep and fastened her belt and straightened her seat.

She mentioned to him, "Oh I am surprised, how time flies!"

Ranbir smiled and looked at her. He deliberately remained quiet as he was confused about his relationships. He thought it was best to let time pass. He hoped everything would fall into place.

Sunanda thought about Ranbir and she felt that he had made love to her in his moment of weakness. He had probably regretted crossing the line. So she decided: once they parted, she would try to forget him, and whatever had happened between them.

4

Ranbir reached his office at ten. He had brought two packets of kalakand from Delhi and he gave one to his assistant to distribute among the staff. In a few minutes, five of his staff members came to his room to congratulate him. He handed his assistant the medallion which he displayed on a pedestal on the table.

Once he was alone in his room, he called up Meera. She picked up her mobile after three rings.

"Hello I am back from Delhi. I have brought a packet of sweets for you."

"Congratulations, I saw you receiving the award on TV. It's a great achievement!"

"Thank you!"

"I saw that Sunanda was with you at the function. You both looked nice together. Ranbir, I am happy for both of you."

He felt exasperated and said in a slight belligerent tone, "I don't know what you mean. She is just a friend!"

There was a pregnant silence. He got a little uneasy and uttered nervously, "Hello, I want to make you an offer for my next film."

Meera was delighted to receive the news. She responded, "Okay, let's meet at Citrus in The Leela at one."

5

Ranbir entered The Leela with the idea of clarifying about Sunanda and his relationship. To his surprise, he found Meera poised and content. The ambience in Citrus was joyful with live instrumental music. They walked to a table on the side of the dais.

The manager presented them with menu cards.

"What do you want to drink? Is Cezanne red wine fine?" Ranbir asked.

"Yes, that is fine with some starters."

Ranbir's phone rang and he saw Sunanda's name flashing on the screen. He switched off his mobile as he didn't want to complicate matters.

Meera could sense his discomfort but decided not to probe.

"No business calls while we are celebrating!" Ranbir clarified.

The waiter brought a bottle of Cezanne with two glasses and put them on the table. He soon brought a plate of barbecued chicken with hot chili sauce.

Meera and Ranbir raised their glasses and said in unison, "Cheers!"

Ranbir was with Meera but his thoughts were elsewhere. He was missing Sunanda and he was worried about her reaction to his phone being switched off.

"What are you thinking?" Meera interjected.

"Oh nothing, I was thinking about the new film."

"Oh yes, It will be wonderful!"

Ranbir called for the menu.

Meera ordered spaghetti with cheddar and Ranbir ordered sol fish in tartar sauce. They savoured their food delightfully as soon as it arrived.

After the main course they ordered sugar-coated donuts with strawberry ice cream for dessert.

The DJ and the orchestra had left and there were only a few diners in the restaurant. She shifted slightly to make place for Ranbir to sit next to her. He changed his seat and moved next to her. He handed her the packet of kalakand. She thanked him for the sweets and once again congratulated him.

There was a pause as they settled down for more discussions over some coffee.

Meera looked into his eyes and asked philosophically, "Life was going on so well, then why did we go off track?"

Ranbir replied poignantly, "We were on the right path till our hearts were pure. We lost our path when we allowed our egos to overshadow the purity of our hearts."

"Can we correct our paths now?"

"Sure we can, provided we have learnt the lessons and are determined to accept the purity of our hearts above everything else."

"Why does God test us all the time?"

"Big structures can be made only on strong foundations. God wants our foundations to be strong so that we can grow."

"Ranbir, I must confess my mistakes before I make any commitment to you."

"It is not required. You have realized your mistakes, so you are on the right path."

"Even then I want to talk about my mistakes as I want to accept you my whole and sole for the rest of my life," she pleaded.

"Go ahead!"

"In the beginning I thought only about you as my lover, my partner and my soulmate. At that time, my life was simple. I was comfortable in my career and I was progressing steadily. Then I became a star. I had a huge fan following and the media hovered around me. I literally got catapulted as a diva. I believed that my stardom was permanent. We had distanced ourselves as I had been overwhelmed by the sponsorship offers, offers for lead roles and you became busy with your work and then went away to Chicago for your workshop. At that time Karan came into my life. He seemed like my prince charming. I thought God was bountiful to me. I got fame, money and a friend. Then after a year of courtship I got the first shock of my life when Karan dropped me like a hot potato to get married to an industrialist's daughter. I was left miserable with a broken heart. Then I got my second shock after the release of *Payal Ki Jhankar* when the film failed at the box office. Suddenly I had lost my star status. Overnight I was replaced by younger heroines. I felt very lonely and dejected. I was in such a miserable state of mind that I felt jealous of your success. To top it, I even felt jealous of my best friend Sunanda, when she accompanied you to the award function." Meera sobbed as she she poured her heart out.

"Thanks very much for your love. I am and I have always been in love with you since the time I had met you." He said without giving her any inkling about his disloyalty. He was prepared to deny the affair in case she mentioned it.

She moved her head towards him and looked at his face. They embraced and kissed passionately.

Ranbir was emotional and he made her the offer, "Meera I am going to make a woman-centric film and I want you play the lead role. You have been the leading lady in all my films and we have good screen chemistry going as director and actor. I am sure the film will be appreciated by the public and it will get you your fan following back."

She was forthright in her reply, "Ranbir, I agree that I have given you one average, one hit and one critically acclaimed film. The last film got you an award, but to be frank with you, my star rating has nosedived. You should look at some new faces; it is easier to make a new face popular rather than trying someone whose popularity has faded."

He was surprised to hear her reply. He knew that it would have taken a lot for her to turn down his offer.

"Meera, I respect you for being so selfless," Ranbir acknowledged.

"You are a good person. I want you to reach the pinnacle of success. I consider your success to be my success," Meera mentioned.

He put his hand around her shoulder; he was feeling on top of the world. He thought that he had finally won her heart. He rubbed his cheeks with hers and looked into her eyes. He picked up a napkin and dried her eyes. They were united again.

She was feeling relieved after opening her heart for him. She had nothing to hide. She had handed over the reins of her life into his hands.

It was already four in the afternoon and Ranbir had been worried about Sunanda because he had switched off his phone. Meera and he had been together for three hours. Ranbir made an excuse to her about some business appointment and both agreed to finally call off their discussions. It had been a pleasant meeting, but Ranbir needed to make a call urgently.

6

Ranbir realized he was in a dilemma. He thought about the sequence of events. He was in love with Meera and first she left him thereby creating a void in his life. Sunanda was his well-wisher. Soon they got intimate, she began to fall in love with him and she filled up the void. Meera – who had left him for Karan – also returned after being abandoned. Meera was so far unaware of Sunanda's relation with him. Ranbir was afraid about her reaction once it was revealed to her that her lover and her best friend were cheating on her. On the other hand, he did not blame Sunanda because she had come to him only after Meera had left him. In fact, Meera had told her that they'd never ever get together. Sunanda could not imagine that Meera's fortunes would change and she would come back in his life.

Ranbir thought it was important to meet Sunanda to find out about her feelings. He called her up.

"Sunanda, I was in a business meeting and could not take your call. The meeting got over a few minutes back. If you are not too busy, can we meet for a cup of coffee?"

"No thanks, I am busy in the emergency ward."

He was a little taken aback by her curt reply as she was always very polite. He feared that she must have come to know about his lunch meeting with Meera.

"Are you okay? You sound a bit edgy."

Sunanda had initially resolved to be aloof but she couldn't bear to be rude.

"I am sorry for being rude. My head of department was a little snappy with me, it is nothing. Can we meet tomorrow evening at seven?" She apologized and made an excuse.

"Will meet you at Legend of China for dinner, if that is fine?" He felt relieved at her agreement and disconnected the line.

He was thinking about the turn his life had taken. He had got fame, reasonable wealth and he had won Meera's heart. These were the goals he had set out for himself and he thought that he could even get married and settle down. However, he felt that his feelings towards her were not as deep as he had initially imagined.

After Meera had surrendered, she had figuratively lost her enigma. He found Sunanda equally attractive. He did not want to let go of either one. After all, Sunanda had surrendered to him despite the full knowledge that he loved Meera. He was trying to gauge what Meera's reaction would be once she came to know about his relationship with Sunanda. There was a chance that she would never know.

The idea of two timing was very tempting and he had a mischievous smile on his face. That was the bane of modern times, he thought to himself.

7

Ranbir spent the next three days thinking about his new film. Once he had resolved to start the film, he made his first appointment with Varun for the script.

Ranbir and Varun met at Natraj Hotel at Marine Drive.

"I want you to write a script for a woman-centric film. It should be in an urban setting," Ranbir said passionately.

Ranbir had a story in mind and he gave the outline. They built the idea and prepared the structure for the story.

Varun confirmed that he would have the script ready in one month.

They parted with the resolve to create an international masterpiece.

Varun devoted all his time and energy in writing the script during the next one month. Finally he informed Ranbir that the script was ready and they could have one more meeting.

Varun had named the film *Noora*. He read from different parts of the script. Ranbir liked the script and paid him five lakhs as advance there and then. Ranbir and Varun had chosen Meera to be the central character of the film. They discussed various aspects of the film, like the star cast, music, cinematography, choreography, costumes and sets.

Ranbir was very happy with the progress and on his way back home after the meeting, he called up Meera.

"Hello, we have the script for our new film ready. Varun has done a really wonderful job. The name of the film is *Noora*. I want you to accept the female lead role."

Meera was very glad to receive his call. She dropped her initial resistance and accepted his offer.

Ranbir believed in taking quick actions. He visited her the next day. They met over a cup of tea and he paid her two crores for the role.

8

Ranbir was seesawing between Meera and Sunanda. He was at his wits' ends romancing both and they both responded to him with love and care. They never gave him any reason to doubt that they were ever in touch with each other or they ever discussed their relationships. He feared that the sword of Damocles always hung over his head. One innocuous comment by either of them could break his relationships with both. It could also put the production of his film in jeopardy.

Ranbir got his warning from an unexpected quarter. Once as soon as he entered his apartment he noticed an envelope sticking outside the letter window.

He opened the envelope, which contained an explicit photo showing him and Sunanda in bed together. He sat on a chair and switched on the fan as his heart was pumping adrenalin into his blood. His fears had come true. He was shocked to see that the photo was taken in the Delhi hotel where they had made love the first time.

There was a small hand written note attached:

"I am in possession of three more equally revealing photographs. I can make the photographs public with grievous consequences to you, your lady love and your public statures. You can prevent it, provided you pay an amount of twenty lakh rupees in cash at Band Strand near Taj Lands End hotel at seven in the evening today. In return, I shall give you all the four photographs, the soft copy and assurance of keeping the matter under wraps."

It was an unsigned letter. Ranbir could not make any guesses from the handwriting. He was clear that the blackmailer meant business because the photograph was not photoshopped. The blackmailer knew that he had a serious affair going on with Meera. He was also aware that she was the heroine of his new film.

He could not discuss the matter with anyone. He even thought of suing the Delhi hotel for spying and photographing their guests. As he calmed down, he realised this was the price he had to pay for two timing. He opened his locker and counted twenty bundles, each of hundred notes of thousand rupees. He placed the bundles in a briefcase and waited for the scheduled hour.

He drove slowly and parked close to Taj Lands End hotel. It was seven and he was waiting to receive a new signal. After two minutes, a white Innova stopped on the other side of the road. A bespectacled, tall, muscular man in black jeans, checked t-shirt and white sneakers got down with an envelope in his hand. He walked straight to Ranbir and showed him the envelope.

Ranbir was convinced that the person facing him was the blackmailer.

"Have you brought all the photographs?"

"Yes, have you brought the money?"

"What is the proof that you will not blackmail me again?"

"It is my word!" the stranger said with conviction.

Ranbir asked for the envelope. There were four photographs and a pen drive. The photographs looked original. In return, he gave the briefcase to the stranger. He held the briefcase, slightly opened it to check, then closed it and turned back towards his MUV. He seemed to be confident that the briefcase contained the full amount.

The deal hardly took five minutes.

Ranbir heaved a sigh of relief. He glanced through the photographs again. He realized that all the photographs had been taken from the same angle. He was sure that at the time of their lovemaking, no one was hiding in Sunanda's hotel room. He guessed that the blackmailer had installed a CCTV camera there.

In film business when the going was good, it rained in money. After Ranbir's national award, the fortunes of his film turned. Two satellite channels had purchased the rights of *Payal Ki Jhankar* to be shown in prime time. He had raked in three crores. The international demand for his film had also picked up and he had netted seven crores from the exports. All film lovers were eagerly waiting for Ranbir's next release *Noora,* which had already been publicized internationally.

He considered the loss of twenty lakhs as inconsequential. He thought it was one of the hazards of dog eat dog world. He considered himself lucky that he had avoided a storm. The bad publicity which those photographs could have generated would have tarnished his image as a well-known director and wrecked his affair with Meera. And last but not the least, it would have also harmed an innocent girl, Sunanda's reputation.

He wasn't sure if the blackmailer could be trusted. He considered the possibility of him making more demands. He let go of the thought, and tried to have faith in the blackmailer's word.

He thought of meeting Sunanda as he wanted to share his experience with her. He dialed her number and checked lovingly. "Hey, can you leave the hospital and meet me?"

She replied, "I will just finish my report and ask my senior. I will call you back."

9

Ranbir and Sunanda chose a secluded corner table at the Lobby Lounge in The Leela. There was reasonable privacy for the guests.

"I was blackmailed today." He broke the news.

"Oh God! What happened?" She put her hand over her mouth as she exclaimed.

He discreetly passed the envelope which contained four photographs and the pen drive towards her.

Sunanda picked up the envelope and carefully looked at the photographs. She looked hassled but still she was in control of herself.

"The blackmailer had installed a CCTV camera in your room. Probably he was one of the guests at the hotel. I don't know how he could gauge that we would be in a vulnerable position there!

"Did you pay the blackmailer?"

"I paid twenty lakhs. I got all the four photographs and a pen drive containing the soft copy."

"That is a huge amount. You should not have paid the money!"

"It would have ruined our reputations. I do not want any harm to come on you!" He deliberately downplayed the effect of bad publicity on his public image as a well-known director. He also completely concealed the effect it would have had on his revived love affair with Meera.

Sunanda was moved by his large-heartedness. She lowered her head and tenderly kissed his hands. She seductively said, "I love you!"

He was touched by her gesture. He admitted that his twenty lakhs ransom was well spent. He tore all the photographs into small pieces and dropped them into the nearest dus bin and slipped the pen drive into his pocket.

He brought his face close to hers and kissed her lightly. They looked into each other's eyes and smiled.

"Love is a many-splendoured thing!" she said.

She looked very pretty and sexy. He thought that it was his love for Meera and his lust for Sunanda's body which had made him heed to the blackmailer.

"What good is money if it can't buy privacy?"

"Are you sure he will not come back again?"

"There exists honour among the thieves; I think he will not come again."

She felt relieved but her next question made him sit up.

"Can we not give respectability to our affair?"

He realized that she was unaware about his romantic involvement with Meera. She considered his relationship with Meera as purely professional.

"I am not ready to settle down."

Sunanda remained quiet and looked hurt.

He realized that he was complicating his life. He had let honesty take the back seat. He touched her hand and asked her to come to his apartment. She meekly agreed.

Sunanda asked suddenly, just as she was about to step into his condominium, "Tell me, do you love me?"

By that time he was already aroused. His conscience had taken the backseat.

He replied automatically, "Yes, my darling!"

The next moment he pushed the door to close it. They were in his bedroom, and he switched on the air conditioner. He gave a mischievous smile and he played Kishore's hit, *"Roop tera mastana, pyar mera diwana, bhool koi hamse na ho jaye!"*

The number suited the mood. They embraced each other and kissed passionately. While in embrace, he asked her, "Why do you want to rush home? You can get ready here and go to the hospital directly from here tomorrow morning?"

"Okay, I will call up Mom and tell her that due to a busy schedule, I am resting at the hospital. I will reach tomorrow evening."

He was pleased with her cooperation. They made passionate love and then fell asleep.

Ranbir got up and saw it was 2.00 am. He was woken up by Sunanda's voice. She was talking to someone on his landline phone. The bedside lamp was on and he heard her defending herself, "Meera, you had told me that you were no longer involved with Ranbir!"

He could not hear what Meera was saying but he could see Sunanda's agony. Her face was flushed. After five minutes of dressing down from Meera, she placed the receiver back as the phone had been disconnected from the other end. His fears had come true. He realized that Meera had suspected him of cheating on her and she had called him at an odd hour to check. When the phone rang, he had been fast asleep and Sunanda had unwittingly picked up the receiver. Meera had a show down with her as she was shocked to learn about Ranbir's treachery and Sunanda's disloyalty.

Ranbir got up to offer some explanation but Sunanda was in shock. He lightly touched her hand but she withdrew it tersely. She hurriedly dressed, picked up her purse and walked out of his apartment.

Ranbir was completely nonplussed as he was at a loss. He didn't know how to handle the situation. He just tossed and turned, trying to get some sleep, but in vain. He knew that he had hurt Meera and Sunanda terribly.

In the morning, he decided to call up Meera. Her mobile rang but it was disconnected after three rings. He knew that she did not want to talk to him. There was a shooting scheduled with her for *Noora* at Filmistan studio at seven in the evening. He feared whether she would come to the set.

Ranbir feared that if Meera didn't turn up, the time of three senior professionals besides his own, the expenses on the set and the salaries of the team members would be wasted. They might also suspect some problems in their relationship. He desperately hoped that she would turn up.

In the evening, everyone waited for her, but to his disappointment, she did not turn up. The set manager came to him and in his presence made a call to her on her mobile. Her phone rang three times and then she picked up. She excused herself by saying that she was not well and that she wouldn't be able to attend the shoot. In spite of the financial loss as well as the time of three seniors, Ranbir felt slightly relieved that at least there would be no showdown. He decided that he would not schedule a shooting till he felt reassured that she would be there. It was eight and the team members had called to wrap up for the day.

Ranbir called up Sunanda. He was worried because he had not spoken to her since the unearthly hour, when she had left his apartment. The phone rang three-four times, but was disconnected. He knew that she was also upset and she didn't want to talk to him. He made his last call to Ravi who lived in Versova. He wanted some advice from him in that moment of crisis.

"Hello Ranbir, how are things?"

"I am fine. Listen, in case you have time, can we meet for dinner,"

"Yes, I can be at the Quarterdeck at 9.30."

He reached the restaurant a little before the scheduled time. He occupied a quiet place and waited for Ravi who was there within ten minutes. They ordered Glenlivet single malt scotch, ice and chicken spring rolls.

"Tell me, what can I do for you?" Ravi asked with the seriousness of a close friend and a guide.

"I have got myself into a complicated situation." Saying that, Ranbir narrated the whole story about his intimacy with Sunanda, Meera's return to his life, his two timing, his film *Noora* with Meera as the lead actor, the blackmail, the showdown and both his lady loves leaving him in the cesspool.

"Many important events have taken place. My first observation is that you did pay heed to my counselling, but for a short while. You displayed maturity by controlling your emotions when Meera was working in your last film while she was also having an affair with Karan. She also acted professionally and you could complete *Payal Ki Jhankar*. The film was appreciated a lot and you also won the award," Ravi said.

"What are you saying?" Ranbir said with a surprised look on his face.

"You are a talented film maker and probably your love affairs manifest themselves into artistic works!" Ravi replied philosophically.

"In a way, I thank God that I have been blessed with so much!" Ranbir admitted.

"Yes, I think providence would shape up your life! Did you see *Slumdog Millionaire*?"

"Yes, Danny Boyle has made a beautiful film in our country and it has been internationally acclaimed."

"Yes, International acclaim is the ultimate goal in film making in our country. To win an international award is the dream for the entire film fraternity in India. You can do that!" Ravi said emphasizing his last words.

"Good idea! Let us aim at that and you can give me the music for the film!"

Ravi's counsel had tremendous effect on his thought process. He made him realize his potential. He was transformed from a weakling to someone who had the power to carve his own destiny.

"You want to continue with film *Noora* or you want to make a new film?

"I think my present film has a great potential. Do you remember Mehboob Khan's *Mother India*?"

"Yes."

"*Noora* is also a woman-centric film. *Mother India* was shot in a rural setting, whereas my *Noora* will be shot in an urban setting."

Ravi was very happy to see Ranbir in his new avatar.

Ravi immediately affirmed, "Yes, I will compose the most memorable music, like AR Rahman did in *Slumdog*. You just get your personal life in order so that you can concentrate on your work."

They parted on a happy note.

10

Ranbir made a call to Meera after breakfast the next morning. He needed to sort the mess he had gotten himself into. The phone rang for a long time and eventually the ringing stopped."

He decided to give her some time. He had not planned for the day, but got ready habitually. He thought he could spend some time with cinematographer Jairaj.

Ranbir walked to his Mercedes M and drove out to meet Jairaj at Oberoi Trident. As he was crossing the National Stadium, he heard his mobile ring. He was happy to see that it was Sunanda. He stopped the car and received the call.

"Hello!"

"Hello, I am sorry for my outburst. I couldn't control myself. I was not aware that you still loved Meera," Sunanda said in a loving voice.

Ranbir loved Meera; he had a kind of fatal attraction towards her. He himself didn't know that why he loved her so much. On the other hand, he found Sunanada sexy and selfless. She had never put any demands on him.

"No, you were right. I have caused you immense grief. I should have been honest." He apologized.

"I should have maintained a distance from you. You had told me that you loved Meera. I should not have tried to seek your love!"

He still had an hour and a half before his lunch appointment.

"Can I pick you up in five minutes? I want to see you," he checked with her.

"Yes, I can manage that. I will be at the gate outside the hospital."

"We can sit in some café. I will drop you to the hospital, then I will proceed for my appointment."

Ranbir stopped the car on the side and Sunanda got in. He was very happy that she had forgiven him.

Sunanda looked thin and her eyes still looked sad.

"How is your mother?" Ranbir tried to break the ice.

"She is fine, thanks! How is your film?"

"We had a shoot the evening of the day you had left but Meera did not turn up. We had to finally cancel it. I have yet not been able to contact her.

"How will you make up with her? I am sorry I am responsible for causing the problems!"

"I wouldn't blame you. It was just my fault."

"How will you pacify her?"

Ranbir put his hand around her shoulders and pecked her on the cheek. They stopped at a cafe. They occupied a centre table and ordered Cappuccino coffee with donuts.

"Meera is a professional. I am sure she would not let her career as an artist as well as the film suffer due to her personal involvement with me! I am going to convince her that *Noora* is targeted for the international audience and the film can win many awards."

"I think you are right. Meera is ambitious!"

"Danny Boyle, an English director, when he made *Slumdog Millionaire* in India, he highlighted the dreams of slum children. That aroused the curiosity of film goers around the world. Satyajit Ray, in his debut film, *Pather Panchali* portrayed the story of two children in a village. His film won many international awards, including Best Human Document at Cannes and an Oscar. The world wants to see India in its real settings. On the contrary, all the commercial films which are being made today are unreal and melodramatic!"

"That is because in India, people go to watch a film to forget about their worries! They don't want to be reminded about their problems in the film."

"You'll have to agree that *Slumdog* was a commercial success! What is important is that the presentation of the film should be slick!"

"Will you not have problems selling an art film to the distributors?"

"This time my film will win an international award first and then it would be launched for the audience globally."

"You have ambitious goals. I wish you all the success."

An hour passed swiftly, they walked out of the café and Ranbir dropped Sunanda to her hospital. He proceeded to the Oberoi Trident to meet Jairaj.

Ranbir wanted that technically the film should be at par with those made in Hollywood. He had included Jairaj as the cinematographer in the team due to his technical knowledge in the field. He had paid him one crore for the job.

The budget of *Noora* was pegged at seventy-five crores. A sum fifteen times greater than that of his first movie. A significant part of this amount was being spent on advertising, the area which he had completely overlooked in that film.

On his return, he got three videos from the HMV store at Kala Ghoda. He had selected three films – *The English Patient*, *Avatar*, and *The Great Gatsby*.

He drove through Marine Drive immersed in thoughts. He had not been able to contact Meera for three days. He knew that besides her relationship with him, she also had the most important part of her career at stake. Was she so hurt that she did not want anything to do with him? He thought of giving her two more days before taking any further step. He thought that the best way to spend time was to watch these DVDs.

11

Meera had watched the National Awards ceremony and the following interviews of the awardees on NDTV. She was quite surprised to see Sunanda standing next to Ranbir during his interview.

She was impressed that Ranbir had complimented Meera for her role in *Payal Ki Jhankar* and had expressed his desire to cast her in his next film.

She had needled Ranbir on his return about Sunanda, saying that she would suit him as his life partner. But after his denial at that time, she let go of her suspicions and decided it was a figment of her imagination. Since she had been deceived once, she had the premonition and her doubts returned when she went to sleep. She got up and checked the time. It was 2.00 am. She gathered all her guts to ring him up on his landline.

The phone rang five-six times and just as she was about to keep the receiver down, she heard a voice on the other end. She immediately recognized Sunanda's voice on the line.

She was aghast as her suspicion about his infidelity and her betrayal was clear.

She immediately gave her a dressing down. She did not mince any words and called her a whore and deceitful. Finally she kept the phone down in disgust.

She got phone calls from Ranbir the next morning but she did not want to speak to him. When the set manager called her from the studio, she excused herself saying that she was unwell.

For two days, she neither called up anyone nor did she take anyone's call. She spent all her time lying down and sulking. On the third day, she called up her friend Veena.

Veena was five years younger to Meera. She was a journalist. She had interviewed her twice and had published good articles.

She found her very understanding. Meera learnt that she was Chief Minister Sudhakar Naik's daughter in her second meeting with her. Veena never flaunted her position anytime in her journalistic career. They had become good friends.

Veena was delighted to receive her call and fixed up a lunch meeting in the Delhi Durbar restaurant.

They got a corner table, ordered Heineken beer with papads and asked the waiter to bring the main course after they had finished drinking.

They got down to business immediately. Meera was candid in expressing her problem to her friend. Veena was sympathetic and quite rational in giving her advice.

"You must consider the facts that he has always chosen you as the heroine of his films, and this time, he is making a special film with you as the central character. You know most of the films in India are male dominated where the heroines are cast as wall flowers only," Veena said candidly.

"I agree with you. Professionally, I have no complaints. He has always been very helpful to me, irrespective of his circumstances." Meera admitted.

"You both are in the glamour world. You cannot apply conservative social norms here."

"We are the same human beings, with the same emotions!"

"Meera, if you do not mind I would like to remind you that you also got involved with Karan."

"Yes, that is true."

"So be understanding, and give him a chance. Most likely he has realized his mistake. As professionals also, you have so much at stake."

"I do blame Sunanda. I thought she was my best friend, and she betrayed me," Meera said bitterly.

"She may have allowed her friendship to turn into a deeper relationship when she learnt that you were hitched with Karan. You should give her a chance as well."

"Your recommendations are worthwhile only if both have mended their ways. It could be that they might not change."

"Wait for a while. Don't jump to conclusions. You have made them realize that you don't like their intimacy. Now you meet them again and find out."

Their tete-a-tete went on for an hour.

In the meantime, they had finished the beer and the waiter had brought salad, makhani daal, keema matar, gobhi and nans.

"Let's eat now!" Veena recommended.

Meera was having her first proper meal in three days. Her anger had melted and she began smiling.

They decided to watch *Delhi Belly* after lunch. The film was a light comedy and they enjoyed it.

12

Ravi and Ranbir had met each other for an early morning walk. Nani Nana park had a lot of greenery and it had a well-paved walkway. They had scheduled to walk and also discuss the hurdles in raising finance for producing *Noora*.

"The distributors have turned down financing *Noora* in the meeting, stating that it is an art film and the public will straight away reject it," Ranbir said dejectedly.

"What is the budget of your film?"

"Seventy-five crores!"

"You have about ten crores. How will you manage funding the remaining sixty-five crores?"

"I will have to go to a bank for finance now, on the basis of my national award."

"The banks do not finance films unless they are produced by some big banners such as Dreamz Unlimited, Rajshri Productions or Mukta Films. You'll have to try a different route."

"I will go for a public issue!"

"The Indian economy is going through a period of recession. This is not the time for a new company to bring out a public issue."

"I will try to collaborate with some big film production companies then."

"I have my doubts. Why not you negotiate with your distributors as you've done in the past?"

"I am making a film with real Indian settings. This is not a commercial film in that sense. I cannot cater to their demands for item numbers and too much action."

"I foresee great difficulties in your raising the finance; I would suggest that you abandon the idea."

"I have already spent eight crores on the project and I have commitments for two crores in the next ten days. If I abandon it now, I lose everything!"

"Why did you start your project without planning for the full finance?"

"I had ten crores, the most prestigious recognition, the cast and the script ready. The rest I left to destiny."

"In the last six months, did you approach anyone for the finance?"

"I have approached two financers who didn't seem to be keen."

"Then it is better that you drop the project!"

Ranbir and Ravi both looked serious. They had completed two rounds of the park and it had also started drizzling. The light shower changed into a downpour within a few minutes. They hurried to the gate. They were drenched by the time they reached the road. Ravi's driver brought the car close to them. They shook hands hurriedly and parted.

Ranbir was feeling low; he knew that he had embarked upon the most ambitious project of his life. He decided that he would put the project on hold for some time till he could make arrangements for the required balance.

He took a shower and changed into fresh clothes. His first call was to Meera.

"Hello!"

"Hello Ranbir, I was about to call you. I am sorry for my aloofness."

Ranbir was very surprised to notice the change in her attitude. She sounded as warm and friendly as she had been during the initial days of their love affair. He was pleasantly surprised by the change in her.

"I am thankful that you have forgiven me. I had called you for another reason. I do not have the finance ready for completing *Noora*, so I am shelving it till I am in a position to arrange for the required finance."

"Oh, I am sad to know that. What is your requirement?"

"Sixty-five crores."

"It is alright, I will wait till you can make the arrangements."

"To be frank, I have reached a dead end. I do not have a clue about where to get the money from."

"In the past also you have faced similar problems and you have successfully come out of them."

"Last time the amount I needed was not as much and my financer and my distributors were partners in my productions. This time my requirement is far more and I am alone."

"Can I be of some help to you?"

"I have to find the solution myself." He was overwhelmed by her offer, but made his point clear.

Meera listened quietly and after a long pause the line got disconnected. She realized that Ranbir was really worried.

Meera received the official letter addressed to all the artists, technical and administrative staff after three days which was printed on Ranbir's production company's letterhead. He as the producer had regretted the stalling of the production of *Noora* film indefinitely due to paucity of funds. The letter further stated that all the staff would be informed as and when the production resumed.

13

"Ranbir, I am coming over to your place and I want to have some discussions with you," Sunanda said.

"Sure, you are welcome."

"I will be there in an hour."

Sunanda took a half day off and drove to his apartment. She wanted clarity about their future.

Ranbir had left the door open. He went to his drawing room and drew the curtains. He switched on the AC and sat down on the sofa. Sunanda walked in after half an hour and sat down next to him.

Ranbir had an unkempt look about him. He had not shaven for the last five days.

"Are you sporting a beard?"

"No, I was feeling a little low and I had nowhere to go, so I stopped shaving."

"Why were you feeling low?"

"I have shelved my film due to paucity of finance. So I didn't have any work."

"How did it happen? You never mentioned that you had such a problem."

"I had embarked upon producing a neorealist film on a big budget. I do not have the backing of my distributors and financers this time."

"It is a tough call, but I am sure you'll find a way out."

"Thanks for your good wishes!"

She came into his arms and put her head on his chest.

"Ranbir, I have come to say goodbye to you. My mother wants me to get married."

She was a young girl, well-settled in her job and she lived with her mother. Obviously her mother wanted her to settle down. Being a young girl, she also wanted to settle down herself. He had been close to her but he had not offered her a proposal for marriage. He felt anguish at the thought of his future without her.

Ranbir realized that life had taken a strange turn. He had come to Mumbai to produce a film and instead he had produced three films. He wanted love, which he got from not one but two beautiful women, and he had had offers for marriage from both of them. Then why did he entangle himself in complications? After achieving his goals, why did he set up higher goals? He could have graciously accepted his lot and could have settled down.

However that stage had passed, and he was in dire financial crisis now. He had invested all his liquid cash in *Noora* and the film was not even one-sixth complete before work came to a halt.

He had never thought of a backup plan. He wondered whether he could do anything besides film production.

"Sunanda, shall we meet after you get married?" He asked with a smile.

"No, once I am married I shall never meet you."

He looked at her wistfully and said, "I wish you a lot of happiness in your married life."

She put her lips on his lips. They kissed lightly and then she got up.

"Do not lose heart. These are testing times. You will get over these challenges!"

"Thanks for your good wishes!"

He walked along with her up to her car. They waved each other goodbye and then she drove her car out to the main road.

Chapter - IV

1

*"*A*mi Bhale Rao Shinde bolto! Ami Chief Minister, Sudhakar Naik cha Personal Assisstant ahe!"* the caller introduced himself as the PA of the Chief Minister.

"Mi Ranbir aho!"

"Tumche Chief Minister milnar bharto!"

"Kathi ani kuthe!"

"Aaj sandhyakale paanch vasta, Sachivalaya Nariman Point."

"Aaho."

"Tumle sathi gadi dhai vasta bhejun."

After that the caller thanked him and disconnected the line.

He was excited to have received the call from the Chief Minister's office. He did not know the purpose of the call but he could guess that it was in connection with his films.

He picked up the DVDs of his three films and kept them in an envelope and sat down thinking about the meeting.

Ranbir had learnt to be patient in life. He had learnt that worrying and fretting, which was a natural response in a tough situation, did not help in any way. He thought that the best way was to plan and execute the chosen path in a disciplined way. He watched the movie *Invictus* directed by Clint Eastwood as he waited.

At 2.30 pm, a middle-aged public relations man arrived to escort him to the CM's office. There was a white Audi with a red beacon on top along with a chauffeur in white uniform waiting for him.

He was guided through respectfully to the CM's office at Sachivalaya. There was a meeting in progress and he was made to wait in a room for some time. He was ushered into the CM's room by his PA exactly at 5.

Sudhakar Naik was sitting on an armed swivel chair behind a large teak table.

He was a well-built middle-aged man. He wore a white kurta-pyjama and brown Kolhapuri chappals. He got up from his chair smiling and walked a few steps to welcome him.

After they shook hands, the CM made him sit on an armed chair opposite him and then sat on his chair.

CM asked him, "What would you like to have?"

He courteously replied, "Tea is fine, thank you."

Within five minutes a peon brought some tea and biscuits; he served them and then left the room.

"I am happy to meet you. Congratulations for winning the national award for *Payal Ki Jhankar*."

"Thanks very much for your appreciation, I feel honoured!" Ranbir acknowledged respectfully.

"You may call me Sudhakar. I have seen only excerpts of *Payal Ki Jhankar,* in my college days I used to be a film buff."

Ranbir felt great talking to a politician and an administrative head, one to one.

"Sudhakar ji, I try to make films with a good story line."

"Ranbir I would like to see your films."

"I have brought DVDs of three films which I have made. You can watch them whenever you like."

"That is very nice; I will watch them when I'm free."

After a slight pause, he continued, "I want you to make three documentaries of fifteen minutes each. They are based on three topics – water, air pollution and energy conservation. I want you to make them because you know how to emotionally connect with the public."

"I am thankful to you. When can I start work?"

"I will speak to the Information and Broadcasting Minister and the Home Secretary in your presence now. They will discuss the details with you."

He picked up the phone and called up both of them.

Ranbir had a meeting at 6.30 at Sachivalaya with The State Information and Broadcasting Minister about the themes of the documentaries and thereafter with the State Home Secretary about the details of the contract.

He was awarded contract for making three documentaries at the price of rupees two crores each. He was assured prompt payments linked with the progress of the films. They assured him full assistance in terms of providing information on the subject and arranging interviews with the concerned officials in the villages and towns in Maharashtra.

Ranbir was excited. The assignment would keep his unit busy for one year, and in the meantime, he could also arrange to finance his film.

2

Ranbir got up early the next morning and after a bath and breakfast, he called up Sunanda.

"I have missed you so much. I wanted to discuss with you some of the recent developments," Ranbir said lovingly.

"I have also missed you. I'll come to meet you at 12."

Ranbir received a call from Meera immediately after that.

She said, "Hello Ranbir, I was worried about you."

Ranbir felt on top of the world as he heard her voice. He replied, "I have some news. I have got an interim assignment from the government to make short films. That will keep our team busy till I can make arrangements for the finance for *Noora*."

"That is a good news, when did this happen?"

"It happened yesterday. I got a surprise call from the CM. He knew about the award I have received and had also seen a few excerpts of our film *Payal Ki Jhankar*. He was impressed with my work, and therefore on his recommendation, I am to produce three documentaries on water, air pollution and energy conservation."

"Can you help me get a good role under another banner so that I can stay busy as well?"Meera asked.

"I will try my best and I will talk to some film producers," Ranbir assured her.

There was a pause and then Meera said, "Ranbir, come over for dinner tonight."

"Thanks for the invitation. I will see you at 8."

Sunanda was at his place at twelve. She was dressed in a patiala suit, dhani kurta with white salwar, green dupatta and green sandals. It seemed that she had taken special care to dress up for the meeting.

Ranbir gently touched her on the cheek and bent down slightly. He gently kissed her cheek and in response she smiled.

"My mom arranged a match for me last evening. I have given my consent. My engagement is on Guru Purab next month and the marriage is eight months from now."

He was surprised to hear of the developments. He realized that probably it would be the last meeting he would be having with her.

He complimented her, "I wish you a happy married life."

She thanked him and said, "Now tell me what is new? You wanted to tell me about some special developments."

"I was personally invited by the CM. The government has asked me to make three documentaries."

"That is very good news. What about your present film?"

"The new assignment will take one year to complete. This would provide interim finance for my production unit till I can make arrangements for sixty-five crores to complete *Noora*."

"Will your star cast wait that long?"

"I have maximum one year provision to bind the cast as per the agreement. Only the discontinuity should not show in the film. Anyway, forget that. What does your fiancée do?"

"He is also a doctor, a cardiologist at Leelavati Hospital. His name is Mayank."

"That is interesting. You'd have a lot to share."

Ranbir had ordered lunch from Yo China. They enjoyed the food together. Sunanda said that she and her Mom were going shopping so she'd leave. Ranbir was left alone and he realized that with the kind of challenges at hand, he would be extremely busy in the coming months.

3

Meera welcomed Ranbir with a hug and a kiss. She looked divine as usual. Ranbir handed her the roses, which he had picked up from the florist. She also kissed the flowers and placed them in a vase on the side table.

They walked to the drawing room. In a few minutes, her maid had brought two wine glasses and a bottle of Chardonnay with nuts and crackers.

Meera opened the bottle and poured the wine for both of them. She kissed the filled glass and handed it to Ranbir. She picked up the other glass and brought it to her lips.

"Cheers!" Meera said with a seductive look.

"Cheers!" Ranbir responded happily.

His mood had changed. He had found her in an inviting mood. He could feel that she wanted to bridge the distances between them.

He brought his face close to her lips and it didn't take long for desire to take over. They locked their lips and kissed passionately. The next moment, she got up and drew the curtains.

They were alone in the hall. She helped him to take off his shirt. He also helped her take off her blouse and he unhooked her bra. He held her breasts and sucked them passionately. They made love on the sofa.

After they were done, they sat close together and sipped more wine. The maid had laid dinner for them. The main dishes had been ordered from Karim's. The food was delicious and while they ate, the conversation shifted to their professional lives.

"For the first time, we would have to work separately," she said

"Yes, I wish I didn't have to stop the work," he said.

"I learnt that KJ has plans to sign a star cast for a romantic film, Ravi ji knows him closely. In case Ravi ji can put a word, KJ might consider me for the female lead." She made a request.

"Oh sure, I will ask Ravi ji to make a request to KJ," he replied assuringly.

When they finished dinner, it was around midnight. He had a challenging day ahead. He kissed her and asked her permission to leave.

She looked a little sad but also understood his challenges. She knew that then onwards, their meetings would be rare.

4

Ranbir and Ravi had met for the morning walk at the Nana Nani park.

"I am glad to hear about your new project," Ravi said as he walked with Ranbir.

Thanks, I have shelved *Noora* for a year and my unit will be busy with the documentaries."

"What about the star cast?" Ravi asked.

"Unfortunately, they will have to wait. But they have the freedom to take up any other assignment during the break. Can you request KJ to consider Meera for a lead role in his next film which I believe is a love story? Ranbir requested.

"I know you love Meera, but by paving the way for her, you are risking to lose her." Ravi interjected with a meaningful smile.

"Oh, I did not look at it from that angle. But I can't do injustice to her. My film is shelved , so how can I expect her to remain idle!"

"Let her find work herself."

"Meera had requested me to approach you. She had said that you know KJ closely and you could put in a word for her."

Hearing that, Ravi's heart softened and he replied, "Okay, I will speak to KJ. Are you sure you'll be able to complete *Noora*?"

"I will do everything to complete my film. When I had come to the film industry, my goal was to produce a successful film. I was successful in producing *Aandhiyan* which was a hit. Then my goal moved to produce a magnum opus, which happened with *Payal Ki Jhankar*. It was a quality film which won me an award too. I have realized that Indian producers don't think big and that is the reason they don't make world class films. It is only a matter of attitude! Now my goal is to produce a world class film," Ranbir said with conviction.

"I agree with you. Now I have over a year to produce outstanding music for *Noora*. In a way, this break is like a blessing in disguise for me. I also want to compose the best music for the world."

They made two rounds of the park before parting.

5

Ranbir and his team travelled to many villages in various parts of Maharashtra to shoot the documentaries. He spent a lot of time in collecting the latest information. He also took help of NGOs, Gram Panchayats, government administration and other local bodies, along with international organizations to understand the ground reality and the government's efforts to tackle the problems of water shortage, water quality, power shortage, and increase in generation capacity, air pollution and its effects. He also met several consultants and plant manufactures in the field of sewage treatment, micro power generation, rain harvesting and effluent treatment.

After eight months of travelling and shooting, Ranbir finally returned home to Mumbai. As soon as he reached his apartment in Mumbai, he saw a card sticking in his letter box. He opened it with a tinge of loss. It was an invitation to Sunanda's wedding. In a moment, the beautiful time he had spent with her flashed before his eyes. He remembered with nostalgia her selfless love and straightforwardness. How happy and fulfilled he had felt in her company! The wedding was scheduled to take place after ten days.

He went to Roop Milan emporium and purchased a Nalli sari for Sunanda and got it gift packed.

"Dear Sunanda, best wishes to you for a happy married life, with love." He wrote on the card.

He dispatched the parcel to her address. He could feel the void which her absence from his life had created. However, the next moment he was well-composed. Partings were inevitable in life, after all.

He switched on the DVD of the clips of his film *Noora*, which he had shot. There were disjointed scenes. The completion of the film would require a lot of hard work and a huge input of funds. Eight months had passed since he had shelved the shooting and he had four months left to arrange for the finance.

Ranbir took an appointment with a venture capital fund company. On his arrival he had his initial meeting with a young manager. They discussed about his film and the return on investment. The manager made him wait and went to meet the chairman. After half an hour, he was escorted into the chairman's room.

The chairman was a middle-aged man in his late forties. He introduced himself as Vineet and shook hands with him. They sat down and began their discussions.

"Mr Vineet, I want to complete a world class film. I want it to win international awards and I want it to have global audience."

"We can provide the venture capital. How much do you require for completing and marketing your film?"

"I need sixty-five crores to complete and market the film."

"How much can you bring in as equity?"

"I have already put in ten crores of my savings and I can further bring in two crores loan by mortgaging my residence."

"How long will it take to complete the film?"

"One year."

"Okay, we will loan you sixty-five crores as venture capital. When your film is ready, that would be the right time for you to come out with an Indian Public Offer to raise seventy-five crores by offering eighty-five percent of the share holding to the public. Lodha and Company can be the marketers of your issue and Bank of Baroda can underwrite it. The issue management would cost around two crores. After the IPO, we shall exit and shall recover our sixty five-crores towards the loan amount and ten crores towards the interest."

Ranbir found that the interest charged by Vineet was reasonable. He looked at the arrangements as a good solution to his problems. He realized that he would be controlling a Public Limited Company with fifteen percent share holding and till that time, he could keep producing successful films.

"How long will you take to give us the loan?

"The paperwork and the disbursement of the amount will take take three months."

"During this time, we shall complete the documentaries. That would be the ripe time to commence the production of *Noora* and the preparations for the Public Issue."

The discussions were successful and they parted in a happy mood.

6

"Meera, I have been able to arrange the capital for completing our film."

"That is wonderful news! We can sit together and plan the shooting dates. I've got news as well. I am the female lead in KJ's *Meherbaan* and have bagged three modelling assignments."

Ranbir was surprised to hear that she had been cast as a heroine in KJ's film. He knew KJ's image. He produced formula films and spent a lot on advertising. As a result, his films invariably did well. In the film circle, he was considered a secretive person and a shrewd film maker.

He couldn't believe that Ravi's recommendation could be so effective. Meera once again looked distant and unreachable because he knew that she was no longer his exclusive heroine. He realized that the break in his film as well as his absence from Mumbai had created a gap between them. He learnt the hard way that to nurture love, actual closeness was also essential.

"Can we meet at The Leela for dinner tonight?"

"Let's meet at the Lounge at eight."

Ranbir decided that come what may, he would not allow any distance to come between Meera and himself. He resolved that his proposed meeting with her would be crucial and he would express his love to her and would propose marriage to her. They could get married immediately after the release of *Noora*.

7

Meera was dressed in a light green gown and green high heels. She smiled when she spotted Ranbir waiting for her at a corner table.

He stood to welcome her and extended his right hand. She gently shook his hand and sat down .

"You look charming!" He complimented her.

"Thanks, you also look nice. You have lost some weight," she responded warmly.

He ordered some sherry for her and cognac for himself.

"It's been a long time since we met!"

"Yes, I had been traveling with the unit to various towns and villages in Maharashtra, shooting for the documentaries. I have finally been able to complete most of the shooting. Dubbing and editing has to be completed. I will be showing the raw clips to the ministry tomorrow."

"That is a new experience, isn't it?"

"Yes, this assignment was God sent. It provided the finance and work for the unit."

"I got a call from KJ three days after I last met you. He interviewed me and quickly selected me for the film *Meherbaan*. Our unit had two shootings in New Zealand. We returned a week back. Next month we are flying to Switzerland."

He noted that he would have to clearly keep her schedules in consideration while planning the shoots for his film.

"Meera, there's something I've been meaning to tell you. I am in love with you and I want to marry you," he said solemnly.

She looked at him poignantly and spoke after a brief pause, "That is wonderful to hear and you know how much I like you, but I cannot get married at this juncture. My contract with KJ does not give me permission to get married for at least two years."

He was a bit disappointed to learn that despite her approval, a legal contract was coming in between their marriage.

He realized that in the meeting, the magic of love was missing. There were practical considerations in the forefront.

8

Ranbir thought it was the right time to meet the CM and show him the progress of the three documentaries. He called up the CM's personal assistant to seek an appointment.

Sudhakar Naik was in a good mood when he met him.

"I have seen the video clips of the documentaries. I must say that you have put in a lot of effort. I have cleared the file and you shall be paid one installment immediately and balance shall be paid after you hand over the final DVDs. When do you think the DVDs will be ready?"

"The editing, dubbing and background music would be completed in one month's time. We can offer the final DVDs in one-and-a-half months from now."

"There is another thing. My daughter is interested in a career in Bollywood. I want you to cast her in your next film."

He was surprised to hear the CM's statement. He couldn't regard it as only a request because of the way his statement was worded. On the other hand, he could not consider it as an order also because the statement was made gently.

He was careful with his reply. "That is a great idea. However, I am in the midst of completing a film and I can start a new film only after a year-and-a-half."

"My remaining term as CM is for two years. In case your film with my daughter as the heroine gets released in one to one-and-a-half years, then I can finance the film."

"I am making a woman-centric film for the global market. I have presently signed Meera as the heroine for the film. I'll have to accommodate changes in the present film to complete it in one-and-a-half years."

"In other words, you would have to substitute your present heroine with my daughter."

"Yes, that would be the case!"

"What is the budget of the film?"

"Eighty crores!" Ranbir replied, adding the advance which he had already paid to Meera and the amount which he had already spent in its production.

"Okay, that can be arranged," the CM said.

"What is the name of your daughter?"

"Veena, she is a journalist. I will ask her to meet you in your office tomorrow."

He agreed and left.

9

Ranbir knew that he had Hobson's choice when the matter was proposed by the CM. He realized that he could not refuse such a high authority in an outright manner, because it was an emotional matter for the CM. He hoped that it would fizzle out as there would be a number of hurdles on the way, which could bail him out from the quagmire.

He was waiting for Veena in his office. He knew that he could never replace Meera. He had yet to see whether the CM's daughter had the potential to be even considered for the role.

Ranbir was taken aback when she walked in.

Veena was about twenty-two. She was tall for an Indian girl and she had thick black shoulder cut hair, a smooth dusky complexion and a lovely face. Her eyes were bright and she had a playful smile. She had an erect posture and good curves. After looking at her, he realized that she was aptly suited to be an actress. In his mind, she had already passed the first test.

"Tell me why you want to be an actor?"

"I am a journalist and I am doing fairly well. Ever since I learnt about your financial problems, I realized that I could use my Dad's position to become the heroine of your film."

He was quite surprised to learn that she already knew about his financial state. He asked her out of curiosity, "How do you know about my financial condition?"

"My Dad had mentioned to me that you had shelved your film and had accepted his assignment."

She concealed the fact that she was Meera's friend and had received all the information from her. Meera had also told her about the scale of the project and his ambition to produce a film for the global audience.

"In fact, I have already found a solution to my financial problem. A venture capital company is lending me for the completion of the film."

"You are a director and your strengths are in the field of art. You should not let yourself be bogged down with the problems of raising finance. Those problems would totally weigh you down."

Ranbir was impressed. He said, "I agree with you regarding the problems of raising finance, and I have often been in desperate situations. But if someone obliges me by financing my film, then he would also have the ownership of the film."

"You can decide whether you want to be known as the director of a world class film or do you want to take the pains of raising the finance and be both, the director as well as the owner of the film."

"In reality, I want to be known as the director of a world class film. It is immaterial whether I am the owner or not. You are right. If I am bogged down by financial pressures, then I may not have the energy or the creativity left."

"You have answered that being owner is not important for you. So it is alright with you if my Dad is the financer."

"That is fine, but the finance comes with strings attached. He wants me to cast you as the heroine and drop Meera."

"I have had a talk with Meera and she has no objection about withdrawing from the film and letting me be the new face. But if you find me unsuitable for the role, then you can reject me," she said with a coquettish smile.

He was aghast to hear her make such a revealing statement.

"You are very suited for the role and I have no reservations on that count. I am only surprised to hear that you've spoken to Meera. I can't believe what you have just said!"

"I've known Meera for two years; we have been friends. She had told me about nine months back that you were facing financial problems. She had requested me to get you some documentaries from the ministry. A few days back she said that she could drop out of the film and I could replace her if my Dad financed the film."

He was surprised to know about what had transpired behind the scenes. He was wondering whether Meera and Veena had conspired to get him the national award as well.

"What you said is mind boggling. I will meet Meera and will let you know my decision."

Veena thanked him, "I will wait for your reply."

She got up and left his room and his office.

Ranbir held his head in his hands. All the information he had received was yet to sink in.

10

"Meera, I had a meeting with your friend Veena in my office half-an-hour back. I want to discuss some important points with you."

"Hello, okay, let's meet at eight for dinner."

"I will be there at the Lounge, see you!" He said and disconnected the line.

He went home to freshen up. He changed into a green striped cotton shirt, dark brown cotton trousers and dark brown shoes.

He found her already waiting for him at the restaurant.

"Hello, you look smart!"

"Thanks very much and you look lovely."

"You have become an enigma. I learnt that you have made a great sacrifice for me." Ranbir didn't mince his words.

"I had mentioned earlier that a new face will be more acceptable to the public. Veena is beautiful and well-suited for the role."

"You did not think about yourself?"

"That was the only way I could help you to arrange for the finance for your film."

"Why did you keep everything a secret from me?"

"I wanted you to hear it directly from the CM and Veena."

"What about you?"

"I am well occupied in KJ's film, so in effect I am managing well."

"Meera, I am afraid there is too much happening in my life. It seems to be full of surprises."

"Life should unfold itself gradually; that's the fun of it! You have the opportunity to embark upon the most important goal of your life. Don't lose the chance."

The meeting went well and they parted on a happy note.

11

Veena as a child was very spontaneous and free. She loved her Dad and Mom. They lived at Colaba Causeway in Mumbai. She had travelled with them to various towns and villages of Maharashtra during her childhood. She spent most of her school vacations with them at the various hill stations like Khandala, Panchgani and Matheran.

Unfortunately, the happiness of the close-knit family was short-lived. She lost her Mom when she was only six years old. One day when she returned home after the school, her Dad informed her that her Mom was unwell and she was in Jaslok Hospital. Her Dad took her to the hospital and she could see her Mom through a glass window lying in the ICU. After that she was sent back home with two attendants. She got the news that her Mom had passed away that very night. When she was brought to the hospital, her dad's eyes were moist. He embraced her and then held her by the finger and guided her to the hospital ward where she saw her Mom's dead body. She cried and her Dad consoled her. She was sent home again. Her Dad returned three hours later, after performing the last rites. That was the saddest day of her life.

Her Dad was very loving and he tried his best to look after her as a single parent.

She studied in J.B. Petit girls' school. Therefore she was never very free with boys. She yearned for boys' company and to fulfill that urge she tried to make some pen pals. When she was fifteen, she got quite close to one of her pen pals, John, who was eighteen and studied political science in Wharton Institute in USA. Later on she realized that he was only interested in her because of her Dad's position in the Maharashtra government.

John had come to India once and had asked her to help organize a meeting with her Dad. She agreed and made the arrangements for his stay in the International Tourist Guest House at Mumbai Central and his meeting with her Dad at Mantralaya.

She went to the Chatrapati Shivaji International airport with her two attendants to receive him. She found that John was very uptight and self-centered. She tried to make his stay in India very comfortable and economical. But he didn't even bother to either thank her or contact her before he left. She felt jilted and yearned for a deeper relationship.

She completed her ISC and joined St. Xavier's Institute for her graduation in journalism. Xavier's was a co-ed college and it had a liberal atmosphere. That's where she got the opportunity to mix with boys.

She had a different take on life after the completion of her graduation. She started her career in Mid Day *as a newspaper journalist. She had lots of outdoor assignments and she made several friends in her professional field. During the same time her Dad did well in Maharashtra politics and he became the Chief Minister. He enjoyed the power and the following. On the down side, due to his busy schedules, he could hardly spend any time with her. He got so very busy in his political career that he met his daughter once in a while during a meal.*

She liked the outdoor life and that propelled her to travel to many countries and to different places in India. Her career in journalism had made her quite bold and adventurous.

Veena had gone to Hotel Retreat, Madh Island in Mumbai for a journalistic assignment once. While about to leave, she saw a man standing with a forlorn expression. He was in a half-sleeved Polo shirt and dark blue denims, smoking a cigarette. He was looking through the glass pane at the garden outside. He seemed to be in his early thirties. He was tall and had a dark complexion. He had a tattoo of a flower on his right upper arm, which showed prominently. She suddenly felt attracted to the stranger.

She seated herself on one of the chairs in the lobby. She stole glances at him. He had a distinct rawness about him. As a journalist she had come across a number of men in her professional life, but that was probably the first time when she realized that her pulse rate had gone up just by looking at someone.

The next moment the stranger abruptly turned his face and glanced at her. She couldn't hide her embarrassment as she was caught staring at him and she instinctively turned her face towards a magazine on the table. The very next moment she was taken aback when she found that the man had sat down on a chair next to hers.

He introduced himself, "Hello, I am Badshah, a captain in merchant navy. I am from the Ala Ulf Baksh Shipping Company. My ship has docked at Mumbai harbour last evening. I wonder if you could be my friend."

She was over the moon; she gleefully extended her hand in acceptance of his proposal and said, "I am Veena. I am glad to meet you and I am a journalist with *Mid Day* paper."

"What brings you here?"

"I am writing an article about the change in Indian tastes. In that reference, I had met the head chef of the hotel. I was about to leave for my office in a couple of minutes." She replied with her best smile.

"If you wish, we can spend some time together at the bar here!"

"Oh fine!"

She accepted the invitation and they walked over to the Oriental bar. The bar was dimly lit and they got a table near the glass window from where they had a nice view of the sea.

He took the lead and ordered a bottle of Jack Daniel's bourbon for both of them. They gulped down half a bottle between them in half an hour.

She found the scotch as well as his company intoxicating. He invited her to his room as she was already tipsy. She agreed readily.

He had a premier suite which had a panoramic view of the Arabian Sea behind the glass window. He closed the door and picked her up in his arms and laid her on the bed. He disrobed and kissed her from top to toe. They made love passionately. She had not experienced such ecstasy before. They lay side by side with their eyes closed holding each other.

When her excitement subsided, she glanced at the time piece on the table and looked at him lying fully awake. She said, "We had quite a session. You are my fantasy. I will come back and we will have good time again."

"It was wonderful. I will get in touch with you tomorrow," he answered.

He walked with her up to the lobby and then she walked up to the porch where a valet brought her car.

12

Ranbir had two ways of raising finance for *Noora*. The first was borrowing venture capital at a high interest, making a world class film and coming out with a successful public issue. He was afraid that he might be caught in the labyrinth which could overshadow his creativity as a director. In that case, he may end up churning out an average film instead of a classic film. The only advantage in this selection was that he would be his own master.

The second option was to accept full finance from Sudhakar. The option entailed giving up the ownership of the film and replacing the heroine. The main advantage in this option was that he was relieved from the hassles of raising finance and he had to focus only on the filmmaking.

Ranbir had thought over the choices carefully. He realized that he required a few points to discuss before he could decide. He decided to have one final meeting with Sudhakar. He called up Veena who was prompt enough to arrange the meeting at 5.00 the same evening.

Ranbir found both Sudhakar and Veena present in the CM's office. He greeted them and took a seat.

He asked without mincing words, "Sudhakar ji, you had mentioned that you would finance eighty crores. Will it be your own money?"

"I am sorry for not clarifying this point. The Ministry of Information will finance the film, but primarily on my recommendations."

He nervously asked his second query, "Would it not be labeled as favoritism towards your daughter as she would be the lead actor?"

"We will keep the information under wrap till your film gets released. If it turns out to be a world class film and she portrays her role well, then there is nothing anyone can say. On the flip side, in case your film fails or she doesn't portray her role well, then it could lead to a scandal. I am a politician and I am sitting on this chair after a lot of power play and probably for a limited time. I have to take that kind of a calculated risk!" He confided in him.

Ranbir could see that behind all that aura of power, there was a doting father. He was satisfied with Sudhakar's reply. The only formality left for him was to sign the contract with the government. He was very happy that he was undertaking a very prestigious big budget project, which would be remembered as a socially responsible film produced by the Maharashtra government. He hoped that the film would be an entry on behalf of the government in various International Film Festivals.

"I have arranged your meeting with the Ministry. I wish you all the best!" Sudhakar summed up.

He was escorted to the office of the Ministry of Information and Broadcasting.

The meeting was successful and he was given two copies of the contract. He read and signed on both the copies. He also got one installment of the payment for the documentaries before he left the meeting.

He called up Sudhakar. "Thanks very much for getting me the sanction of eighty crores for the production of *Noora*. I am ready to make the film and cast Veena as the female lead."

"I am glad to hear that. She is not here in my office. I suggest that you give her the good news yourself."

13

Ranbir got a call from his office saying that Veena had called up. She had left a message for him that she would be reaching his office at 11.00 the next day.

He reached his office well in time.

She was escorted to his room upon arrival.

He welcomed her with a broad smile and asked his assistant to bring in tea and snacks.

"Oh my, I am getting a big treat!" she sat down with a bright smile.

"I have had meetings with Meera, your Dad and the Minister of Information and Broadcasting. Meera has gladly offered the lead role to you. She said that she has the lead role in KJ's film, a few modelling and sponsorship assignments to keep her busy. Your Dad has arranged the finance for the film through the Ministry of Information. I have chosen you as the new heroine of *Noora*. I know you have been greatly responsible for the turn of events. It is a lucky day for both of us and we must celebrate." He informed her happily.

They both helped themselves with laddoos, samosas and tea to cement their partnership as the director and actor. He explained the script of the film *Noora* and told her about the team members.

"I will send you a copy of the script tomorrow. I will also arrange your meetings with the main cast, music director, cinematographer, choreographer, cameraman, script writer and the rest of the team. We shall be able to start shooting in exactly one-and-a-half months' time. I shall complete the documentaries in the mean time."

"What do you think I should do to prepare for the role?"

"You should read the script and visualize the highlights well. I want you to be a methodist actor. Get into the character of Noora. Jairaj the cinematographer will give you good tips for your role. I will also give you the DVD of the clips, which have been shot with Meera. You may get some ideas from there, but don't get awed by anyone, we work with an actor's natural style."

She thanked him and bade him goobye. It was a special day for her. She had got the opportunity of her lifetime. She had got the break in a world class film and she desperately wanted to celebrate the news with Badshah, her boyfriend.

Ranbir reflected about his meeting with her.

He thought deeply about how he could create something outstanding. On his way home, he picked up a DVD of *Eyes Wide Shut*. He was impressed by Stanley Kubrick's direction and spent the afternoon watching the film.

14

Ranbir received a phone call at four. He was surprised to notice that Sunanda was on the line.

"I have received your gift. I want to wear it for you tonight. It has been over eight months and we haven't met at all."

"Yes true, come over for one last time before your wedding."

"I will meet you at your place at eight."

Ranbir took a bath and changed into a checked cotton shirt and brown cotton trousers. He gave his helper the evening off and ordered dinner from Legend of China.

At eight, Sunanda walked in, wearing the blue Nalli sari. She wore a gold necklace, gold bangles and long gold earrings. He noticed that she had lost some weight during the last eight months.

"You look delectable," he commented with a twinge of regret.

"Thank you very much. I love the sari."

"Let's have some wine."

She helped him get the wine glasses and arrange the cheese cubes in a platter with forks.

They carried the glasses and sat next to each other on the sofa and raised the glasses to their lips.

"You are getting married tomorrow. Are you excited or nervous?"

"Mayank is an understanding person and he loves me. We have planned to fly to Delhi after four days and take a connecting flight to Leh for our honeymoon. So yes, I'm pretty excited."

He cupped her face and pulled her towards him for a kiss, but she smiled and withdrew.

"What is the matter?"

"Nothing. I want to be true to my partner. I regard you as my friend."

He was a bit sad to find that she was pretty steadfast in her attitude. He was helpless before her.

They had finished the wine bottle while talking about the changes in the production of *Noora*.

She helped him in heating the food and serving it on the dining table. After dessert, they cleared the table and washed up together.

She looked at her watch and got up to leave. He walked her to her car. He put his hand around her shoulder, brought his face close to hers and wished her a happy married life. They waved to each other and she drove the car out of the exit gate.

Ranbir walked home slowly with a feeling of nostalgia. Once home, he closed the main entrance, switched off the lights and got into bed. After about half an hour, he heard his landline phone ring.

He picked up the receiver and said, "Hello".

There was a pause and then in a moment his peace was disturbed.

"Hello, I have your and your lady love's photographs. You can find the two photographs in your letter box. She is getting married tomorrow. If you want to save her reputation, then meet me at the same place at Band Strand at seven in the evening tomorrow with twenty lakhs in cash." The caller said in a hard tone.

It was the same blackmailer! Ranbir kept the receiver on the table and rushed to check the letter box. There was a white envelope with two photographs.

In the first photograph he and Sunanda were sitting on the sofa. He was leaning towards her to kiss her.

The photograph must have been taken the same evening in his own apartment. There was someone else who had sneaked into his apartment. The intruder must had left when they were busy eating.

He guessed that the second photograph was taken near her car about forty-five minutes back. In the photograph, he had his arm around her shoulder, his face close to hers.

The photographs had the time as well as the date printed on them. Ranbir knew the photographs could ruin Sunanda's married life, which was yet to begin. The scandal would also affect his image.

More than his image, he was worried about her happiness. He had a good amount of money which he had received as instalment for the documentaries. Ranbir was very protective about Sunanda and therefore he didn't want any upheavals to rock her married life. He decided to go and pay off the ransom the next day.

15

Ranbir put twenty lakhs in a briefcase and left for Band Strand. He reached at five minutes to seven and parked his car at the same spot before Taj Lands End hotel. At seven, a white Innova stopped on the other side of the road and the same bespectacled blackmailer came out and stood with a white envelope in his hand. The man handed over the envelope containing a pen drive and two photographs. Ranbir just had a glimpse inside the envelope and handed him the briefcase. The man didn't bother to check the cash and got into the car. He started the engine and drove away.

Ranbir drove to his office. He had an extra key to the entrance. He opened the office, switched on the light, the air conditioner and sat down on his chair. He was thinking about Sunanda who was getting married at that moment. He was happy that he had been able to avoid a crisis in her life by paying the ransom. His first experience of ransom had convinced him about the characteristics of the blackmailer.

Ranbir was not morally upset that he was paying the blackmailer the second time. He thought that he was making so much of moolah that such hazards were unavoidable. He was also concerned about his own safety because he was convinced that someone knew his moves and whereabouts. Someone could even sneak into his apartment; he could easily be attacked. He realized that he immediately needed security. He decided to engage a good private agency to protect himself against the stalker.

He zeroed in on Group 4 security on the first page of results. He examined the website of the security agency. They had good credential rating and they had a list of satisfied multinationals and high profile individuals. He called their office and asked them to depute two strong guards in plain clothes with licensed revolvers for his security against a suspicious stalker. The call was received by a manager who provided him with the details of the guards. He confirmed that the two guards would be with him within an hour. He added that there would be change of duty after twelve hours and two other guards would replace them. They would be on duty by rotation.

He decided to complete some official jobs while he was in the office. He called up Vineet from the venture capital firm on his mobile to tell him that he would not be requiring their services.

He made his next call to Subway and ordered a sandwich with brown bread, salad, and chicken tikka along with diet coke.

By the time his dinner was over, two guards in plain clothes had arrived. They showed him their identity cards and briefed him about the arrangements. He was satisfied and was escorted by the two guards to his apartment soon after. One guard drove his car and the other sat with him in the back seat. The guards had been trained to remain alert and keep a watch against any lurking danger. They remained quiet unless spoken to. They reached his residence in half-an-hour. He showed the guards his home. They carefully examined the whole place. Once they were satisfied that everything was safe, they left him in the master bedroom. The guards were quiet by nature and focused on their own job. They would deter the stalker against any further evil designs. In a short time, he forgot about their presence.

Chapter - V

1

"The consignment is due to arrive at Daman creek tonight. You go with your four armed hitmen. You know the password and you have met the Afghan sellers. First check and take the delivery and then make the payment," Chhota Rajan ordered.

"Yes, Boss, I will come to Hotel Victoria to collect the cash," Badshah replied.

"Come at twelve in your Innova today. Manya will hand over four crores cash in a suitcase. You deliver the briefcase containing one hundred sachets of heroin at the same time here tomorrow."

It was already eight and Badshah had just got out of bed when he had received Chhota Rajan's call. Rose, his escort was still asleep on one side of the bed. He slapped her on the bum and woke her up.

He instructed her while she was still half awake, "Get up! I have to get ready and leave in forty-five minutes. I have to report for work by twelve."

He called up Robert, Peter, Samuel and Joseph who were his accomplices. Chhota Rajan paid ten percent of the consignment value to him and he paid forty percent of his commission to them.

He packed his suitcase; paid Rose twenty grand and both of them left the suite.

He wheeled his suitcase to the billing counter at the lobby and checked out. The bill was for one lakh and twenty thousand rupees which he had spent on his drinks, food and stay in just five days.

Overall, he considered his stay as quite satisfying. He thought Rose was good, but Veena was far better.

Badshah reached his apartment at Kalina in an hour. He unloaded his luggage and picked up his revolver and his raincoat before leaving for Hotel Victoria to collect the cash. His four accomplices joined him outside hotel Victoria at quarter to twelve. They had come in their Tavera, all set for the assignment.

Chhota Rajan's deputy, Manya handed him the suitcase containing four crores cash.

He along with his accomplices left for Daman. The suitcase containing four crores was with him. They still had seven hours' time to reach Daman beach. They decided to take a break to enjoy a few drinks at the Regent hotel on the highway.

Badshah calculated that in the deal, after the delivery of the drug consignment to his boss, deductions of commission to his accomplices and other expenses, he would make a sum of twenty two lakhs. On the other hand, he had made fifty lakhs blackmailing Ranbir. That was the net amount he had made after blackmailing Ranbir, advances he received from KJ and the cut he paid to Chhota Rajan.

He thought that in the drug business he was dealing with hard core criminals, who were all trigger happy. He had a bigger threat from police of Maharashtra and Union territory of Daman. On the other hand, while blackmailing he dealt with a few soft targets and just Mumbai police. He summed up that blackmailing was far more lucrative and easy than the drug business.

He decided to wriggle out of the drug dealing and to focus only on blackmail in the future. He calculated that they would be at the beach in two hours and would have to wait for the arrival of the motor boat. There was a remote possibility of police action. He was confident that they were prepared to defend themselves against mild skirmishes. There could be real danger only if the police had received prior information.

They arrived on the beach about an hour before the scheduled time. They parked their MUVs with a gap of about twenty metres along the beach and remained seated inside. It had started raining and consequently the visibility was poor. They put on raincoats and intermittently switched on the wipers to clear the windscreens. After a long wait, they saw a motor boat which was steadily ferrying towards the beach. Badshah saw the signal light and responded with his Innova lights. In five minutes, the motor boat had docked about thirty metres away. He could see the silhouette of six men walking towards them in the pouring rain. They were Afghans. The leader carried a briefcase in his right hand and the rest of the gang members carried revolvers.

Badshah and his four accomplices came out of the MUVs. He was holding the suitcase and was leading them.

Badshah recognized the Afghan leader because he had taken the delivery of drugs from him in the past. The rest of the gang members were new faces.

Badshah and the Afghan leader waved with their free hands to show familiarity and then they exchanged the briefcases. Both sides briefly inspected their items and satisfied, parted hurriedly as it was pouring.

Badshah was relieved the transaction had gone well and they began their return journey to Mumbai.

2

Veena had tried to contact Badshah for six days. She visited Hotel Retreat twice during those days, but she was told he was away.

On the seventh day, she was taken by surprise when she received his call.

"Hello, my girl," Badshah coolly said.

Veena was first upset because he had not taken her calls for six days and had not responded to her messages, which she had left at the hotel.

She had softened because he had finally contacted her, "I am fine. I wanted to meet you to share some good news."

"Let's meet at the Madh Island beach at eight in the evening?"

She was delighted and happily agreed.

Veena was excited. She did her day's work mechanically and at six, she left for Madh Island. She spotted his silhouette when she got out of her car at the beach. The fierce sea waves lashed on the sandy beach. The moonlight shimmered on the sea surface and the beach looked idyllic.

She ran and embraced him as soon as they met.

"I have got a major break in life. I have been selected for the female lead role in a film under the national award winning director Ranbir." She happily gave him the news.

Veena found him looking a changed person in the dim light. She was taken by surprise by his peculiar hard expression. He had a sneer on his face and he looked sinister. All of a sudden, the whole place looked eerie.

Badshah put his hand in his pocket and drew out an envelope. There were four sexually explicit photographs, which showed Veena embracing a man. The photographs had been shot in such a way that they exposed only her. The man was unidentifiable in the snaps. Those were taken when she and Badshah had made love a few days back. She looked at him realizing her vulnerability. She had suspected that he had spiked her whiskey at the Oriental.

"What do you want? Who are you?" She questioned with a puzzled expression.

"I want fifty lakhs in exchange of the original photographs and the soft copy." He threatened with a malicious look.

She shouted in disbelief, "You can't do that!"

"I will do just that and if you do not pay, I will send the photographs to the media." He stated with a cold expression.

She felt as if she was drained of all the energy from her body. She was convinced that he would execute his threat.

She relented, "I will arrange for the the cash tomorrow evening at this time. Meet me here with photographs and the soft copy."

"That is better. And don't try any tricks otherwise you'll be responsible for the consequences." He threatened her again. He was satisfied that she looked scared.

She walked towards her car in quick strides. She saw that he was walking towards a white Innova parked near a cluster of palm trees.

She unlocked her car and sat on the driving seat. She wiped the perspiration from her face with the help of a tissue. She switched on the engine and the air conditioning. She feared that if she did not pay the amount, all her dreams of being a heroine would be quashed.

Her Dad had provided her with all the luxuries, but not that kind of cash. She made good money as a journalist but she spent it all on foreign jaunts. She could not ask her Dad for the urgent requirement of such a large sum because she would have to answer too many questions.

She thought of asking Ranbir for the cash and making him her confidante. She could ask him to inflate the cost of film production and get the same reimbursed by the ministry.

"Hello Ranbir, I want to meet you immediately." She called him while driving.

"Hello, come home." He replied and gave her his address.

When she reached his apartment an-hour-and-a-half later, she saw two security men in plain clothes at the entrance, who allowed her to go in the apartment.

He was waiting for her in the drawing room. She closed the door while entering and said, "This is confidential. You pay me fifty lakhs and get the same back by inflating the cost of film production."

"I can't do that!" He was puzzled with the sudden announcement.

"You can. After all, the cost of the film can vary."

"I have already signed a contract and the budget has been fixed.

"There is a cost variance clause. It is a standard feature and if it is not there, then I will get the same added in your contract, but I need the money by tomorrow evening." She said looking pale as if her blood had been drained out.

"What is the problem? Tell me." He asked her.

"I am being blackmailed by a man. His name is Badshah. I made the blunder of having sex with him. I did not know that he had spiked my drink and he had kept a camera on when we made love. He has four photographs to blackmail me. My future as a heroine is at stake." She said despairingly.

Ranbir looked shocked; he also thought that Badshah could be the same blackmailer. Ranbir was convinced that he knew that Veena was the heroine of his new film and that she was also the

CM's daughter. He knew that she could pay such a large sum in just one day.

"Okay, I will arrange the money, but I will go with you to get the photographs and the soft copy."

"No, he will get unnerved and may not give me the photographs."

"The blackmailer knows me, because in reality, I am his target."

" What!" She was surprised to hear that.

Ranbir told her all about the blackmailer and how he had been targeted.

"The blackmailer is aware about your getting the film contract and he also knows that you have the resources to pay off the ransom within a single day."

There was a silence for a few minutes as both were trying to guess the sources of the leak.

"Can you describe him?"

He gave the details of the blackmailer, his Innova number and his mobile number.

"He probably thinks that I will not talk about the blackmail to you."

"It is likely because otherwise he would not have struck within a short gap of just four days. Last time, he had struck after a gap of ten months. The blackmailer is most likely from the film industry or he has his partner there, because he knew the details about my new film."

"I will go and pay off the ransom and collect the photographs. You do not show yourself."

"I will discreetly follow you and park my car at a distance."

She felt more secure and agreed to his suggestion before they parted.

Veena reached his apartment at five in the evening the next day. He had given leave to his security staff for the day. She got fifty lakhs in a large briefcase from him. They discussed their plan and then she drove towards Madh Island. He followed in his car, albeit maintaining a gap. Both were careful so that they were not being tracked by Badshah's white Innova.

Two kilometres before Madh Island, Veena halted and waited for Ranbir's car. It was 7.30 pm. She saw his car slowing down at a distance. She gave him a signal with her head lights and then proceeded slowly for the rendezvous. Ranbir followed at a distance. She parked her car on the roadside and took out the briefcase. She walked with it towards the beach. Ranbir stopped his car at a spot from where he could see her and remained seated inside.

It was five minutes to eight and the air was still. The sky was overcast with dark clouds. At eight, she saw the silhouette of Badshah approaching her. He walked in quick strides, holding an envelope in his right hand.

When he was a few meters away, she pointed towards the briefcase. He raised his hand to show the envelope. She handed over the money to him and in exchange he handed over the envelope. She opened it and found four photographs and a pen drive in it. He quickly opened the briefcase, looked at the bundles and walked back. They did not exchange any words and she stayed behind. The moment she noticed that he was not looking at her, she took out a Wesson .38 Caliber pistol from her blouse and shot him. The bullet pierced his back and he fell to his knees. He immediately looked back with a shocked expression, his body contorted in pain. He gathered all his strength and lunged forward to grab her pistol. She didn't give him the opportunity to come near her. She pressed the trigger twice and shot him through the chest and the stomach. He fell with a thud to the ground; for a few moments his torso trembled, and then it became still.

Ranbir was watching both of them from behind a tree at a distance. As soon as he heard the shots, he ran towards them. By the time he reached the spot, he saw Badshah's slain body on the beach and Veena holding the pistol in one hand and the envelope in the other. The slain body still had its right hand on the handle of the briefcase. He saw that the beach was deserted and no one else had heard the shots or noticed them.

"Please pick up the briefcase," She said.

"Why did you murder him?" Ranbir asked with a shocked expression.

"He would have come again!" She replied flatly.

He was nervous but he marvelled at her guts. He took a few steps and picked up the briefcase.

"Ranbir, you can go unscathed. Let me handle this alone!"

"No Veena, we are in it together."

"What do we do with his body and his Innova?" she asked.

"I will take the keys from his pocket and bring his Innova here. We will dump his body in the MUV and abandon or destroy it somewhere."

Veena emptied all the contents from Badshah's pockets. She had his wallet, car keys, a latch lock key, mobile and some change. She handed Ranbir the car keys and switched off the mobile. She took out the sim and threw the handset and the latch lock key into the sea.

He left the briefcase on the ground and ran with the keys towards the Innova.

She looked around; it was dark, barring the scattered moon light through the clouds.

She slipped on the safety catch and slipped the pistol inside her blouse. She looked at the dead body. She removed the shirt from the dead body and used it to wipe the blood that had trickled to the sand. She kept the dry part of the shirt on the wounds. She looked at the dead man's face and spat on it.

In about five minutes, Ranbir had brought the Innova near the dead body. He opened the back door and both of them lifted the body off the ground and shoved it inside. He drove the MUV up to her Vento. She kept the envelope, Badshah's wallet and the briefcase below the side seat and took the driving seat.

Ranbir drove the Innova and Veena followed him in her car for almost ninety minutes. Finally they reached a hilly area. He drove the Innova up to a peak and then brought it to a halt. She also brought her car to a halt. She got out and walked to the Innova He switched on the engine and moved the MUV, he changed the gear to first and while it was moving, he jumped off. The Innova moved ahead and within a minute it climbed the cliff and then toppled over. They heard the sound of the vehicle hitting the rocky slope twice, followed by a blast and then they saw red flames as it had caught fire. Both of them ran towards the Vento and got into it. She sped on the side road as Ranbir looked towards the accident site. They knew that by then the local habitants would have heard or seen the explosion.

"I think we have had a clean escape. Now let us try to forget our meetings with the blackmailer as a bad dream and lead normal lives." He suggested.

"I agree with you. I will try to erase his memory as a bad dream."

They drove back to Madh Island where Ranbir's car was parked.

She stopped and he got off. He walked towards his car and got into it. She drove ahead and he followed.

Veena parked her Vento with the other parked vehicles near his apartment and waited for him. Once he was there, they walked together to his apartment.

She handed him the briefcase containing the cash and sat down. He asked her, "Should I make a drink for you?"

She said, "I should go home and relax. We've had a tiring day; will talk tomorrow."

He did not press her and she walked back alone to her car and drove home.

He was tired and he went for a shower. He changed into night suit and went to sleep. The happenings of the evening seemed like a bad dream.

3

Ranbir had uneasy sleep as he tossed on the bed. He once got up with a start. He had a nightmare that the police had tracked them. They had been handcuffed and taken to prison.

He opened his eyes to find that he was perspiring and his heartbeat had gone up. He looked around with relief that he was in his own bedroom. He tried to reassure himself that Badshah's body along with the MUV would have burnt at the isolated place in the hilly terrain. He was sure that there was hardly any chance of the police getting to them.

He went to the washroom, did some deep breathing exercises a few times and splashed his face and head with cold water. It was 3.00 am. He decided to lie down for a few more hours and then call Veena.

He went back to bed and he could rest for just about two hours. He finally got up and made a cup of tea for himself and switched on the television. He sighed with relief that there was no news regarding the murder or the burnt MUV on any channel.

He went for a shower and changed into fresh clothes. He took out the briefcase and checked the cash inside, which he found intact. He transferred the cash into his safe and picked up the briefcase. He had to discard it.

It was 6.30 am. He walked with the briefcase to his car and drove out. He saw a big garbage bin on the roadside. He stopped his car and slowly walked towards the bin. He looked around and then tossed the briefcase inside. He was satisfied that nobody had seen him discarding it. He walked back, got into the car and drove off. He called Veena.

Her mobile rang twice and then she picked up. After a pause he asked her, "Is everything OK?"

She sounded confident and replied, "Yes, we have been successful in getting rid of the leech."

He was relieved to hear her and mentioned, "It has been a successful operation, I must admit."

"Can we meet?"

"Yes, can you pick me up from Gateway of India in another half an hour?"

Ranbir reached in time and parked his car at the Gateway of India. He walked to her and they exchanged smiles. She looked slim and athletic in stretch pants, a halter-necked top, and skids.

"I was just wondering, there could be an inquiry from Hotel Retreat when Badshah does not return. At the accident spot, the police could find clues which could get them his details. They might learn that he was a blackmailer and some clue could lead them to us." He shared his fears.

"The police can track us, so we need to have solid alibis ready. We should also be able to establish that we were not together at the time of the murder or the accident." She spelt out the precautionary steps.

"What did you do with the pistol? If the police discover the dead body, they would know that the victim was shot dead before his body was loaded into his Innova and it was deliberately pushed over the cliff. They would look for the murderer as well as for the murder weapon."

"I have my pistol in my locker in my bedroom. It is a licensed pistol. In case there is a ballistic report, then it is possible to link his death to me."

They both thought over it.

"There is no chance of the police discovering so much. I am sure the explosion would have burnt the dead body to cinders." He said optimistically.

"I don't think the police will be able to reach us. We can relax," she said smilingly.

"You are a very spunky young woman and you have got both of us out of a dangerous situation."

"I was over the moon after getting the film role. I was also under his spell for a while. When he revealed his hideous side, I saw my world crumbling. I had decided to murder him immediately after I learnt from you that he was a seasoned blackmailer."

"It is good that you did not share your plans with me. I might not have been able to handle it."

She accepted the compliment meekly.

They parted company and he drove to his office. He met his body guards at his office, who were back on duty after a day's rest. He thought that he could pay the agency in advance for the month and stop their services. Veena and he had gotten rid of the stalker for good.

Ranbir spoke to the manager of the company who told him what he had to do. He wrote a check and handed it to one of the guards. He conveyed the manager's instructions. Both the guards saluted him and left his office. He did not discuss about the discontinuation of his private security arrangement with his other staff.

He got busy with the editing of the documentaries. He worked alone till the afternoon. He felt a little hungry as he had not eaten since last evening. He ordered a small pizza from Pizza Hut. He called for the newspaper and leafed through it. On the third page he saw the photograph of Badshah's burnt Innova.

The accompanying report mentioned, *"A charred Innova MUV with a burnt body inside was found at Nalasopara. By the time locals reached the accident spot, the fire had engulfed it. The fire brigade and the police were called to the accident spot. The police have been able to track the details of the owner of the Innova. It belonged to a person named Badshah Unus from Kalina. The police have confirmed that it was his charred body which was found in the MUV. The victim was an underworld drug dealer and was involved in many nefarious activities. The police is investigating whether it is a case of an accident or he was murdered by some of his enemies."*

He was relieved to learn that according to the news report, the police did not suspect them for the murder. He felt relaxed.

He immediately called Veena and shared the newspaper report and his personal views on it. "It looks that the explosion and the ensuing fire burnt the Innova and Badshah's body. The police have tracked the Innova to Badshah. He was a drug dealer and he had some record of crimes and the police suspect the cause of his death to be reckless driving under the influence of liquor or some underworld retaliation. The media as well as the police seem to be unsympathetic towards him because of his anti-social record."

"I am glad that we acted on our instincts and we could avert a perpetual threat. He would have been bleeding us through blackmail on a regular basis."

He agreed with her and bade her goodbye.

4

The police had taken photographs of the burnt Innova and sent the charred body and samples from inside of the charred MUV to the forensic lab.

Inspector Jatin had just received the ballistic report of the murder. He learnt that Badshah had been shot thrice from a Wesson .38 Caliber pistol. The forensic study provided a few more details. He learnt that the murder was committed at a different place, which was most likely at a beach because there were specks of sand in the Innova. His body was dumped in the dicky of the Innova and it had been driven off the hill deliberately.

The report also mentioned that the man's mobile, wallet, apartment key had been removed by the murderers because they could not get any traces of these items from the charred MUV. Probably two or more persons were involved because another car would have been needed for their escape.

Jatin went to Badshah's apartment at Kalina at night. The three-bedroom apartment had been locked by the police earlier in the day as he had lived there by himself. He ordered the staff on duty to unlock the main entrance. He entered the apartment alone and switched on the lights. He conducted a thorough search. He found a cupboard in the master bedroom. He unlocked it and inside, he found a briefcase. He took photographs to get the finger prints and then he opened it. He found a lot of cash inside. He also found a CCTV camera inside the cupboard. He switched on the camera and he found a number of photographs of persons either in sexual acts or in intimate positions. The subjects in the photographs didn't seem to know that they were being filmed.

Jatin was convinced that Badshah was a blackmailer and those people in the photographs were most likely his victims. He guessed that the cash was received by Badshah either as the blackmail payoff from his victims, rewards from his bosses or it was his commission in the drug dealings. In the second bedroom, he saw a laptop and a colour printer. He found some edited photographs which were grouped separately in one folder in the laptop. He knew that the persons in the photographs were his targets as well as the likely murderers who took revenge.

In the drawer, Jatin found Badshah's .45 automatic Colt revolver. He considered it ironical that he did not carry his revolver on that fateful day. He probably did not expect being attacked. Perhaps he knew the killer well.

5

Inspector Jatin had been able to get the identities of the persons in the photographs through a big database of people and an interactive software in his head quarter computer section. Out of the four sets of photographs, the first set had photos of well-known film producer cum director, Ranbir and a lady doctor, Sunanda. They had been clicked in the act of love making. The second set contained photographs of Veena, a young journalist in *Mid Day,* the daughter of the Chief Minister, Sudhakar Naik, and Badshah making love. The photoshopped pictures showed only Veena in the act of love making whereas Badshah's face was blurred. Obviously she was his target. The third set had photographs in which he was sitting with film producer KJ. In the first photograph he was holding the CCTV camera while KJ was speaking. In the second photograph he was receiving cash from KJ, which looked like some payment for a deal. Jatin understood that he was also KJ's agent. KJ being Ranbir's rival must be interested in tarnishing

Ranbir's image. The fourth set showed him standing with Chhota Rajan, and his deputy Manya.

Jatin realized that Badshah was a smart operator and he preserved not only the photographs of his victims, whom he blackmailed, but also the photographs of his bosses to pressurize them in case they tried to ditch him. Alas, in spite of his impeccable planning, his life had been severed by either his victims or his bosses.

Jatin guessed that Badshah sometimes acted on his own by deceiving his bosses. He was blackmailing people without Chhota Rajan's full knowledge and he had threatened the victims and collected the money without KJ's knowledge.

Jatin found out that Sunanda had got married six days ago. He checked her home page on Facebook where he found the newly-married couple's photographs. The dates shown on the photographs and the date and time of Badshah's murder exonerated her of any role in his murder.

He also got the information from police files that Veena had a licensed Wesson pistol. Veena and Ranbir could be the murderers.

Jatin consulted the public prosecutor, Ajit and briefed him on the findings.

"The earlier report that Badshah got shot by some of his enemies in the underworld is doubtful. KJ, the film producer wanted to tarnish the image of his rival Ranbir and he fixed Badshah for getting his private photographs. Badshah was successful in getting the scandalous photographs, however he got smarter and blackmailed him directly to get more money, without KJ's knowledge. He was blackmailing three persons: Ranbir, the film director; Sunanda, a doctor in Breach Candy hospital, and Veena, a journalist and CM Sudhakar Naik's daughter," Jatin briefed him.

"It is also possible that he could had been murdered by KJ or even by Chhota Rajan with whom he fallen out as he was deceiving them," Ajit pointed out.

"Yes, that is also possible. I will work on that angle." Jatin replied.

"You should be careful because you are accusing the CM's daughter, a well-known film director and a respectable doctor. If you cannot stick the murder charges, then you will sure face their wrath." Ajit cautioned him.

Jatin felt jittery because he knew that he was playing with fire by going after high profile people. He was also not sure whether Ranbir and Veena knew each other to team up to murder their common enemy. He decided to first interrogate Ranbir.

Jatin reached Ranbir's apartment. A helper opened the door. He was made to wait in the corridor. Ranbir appeared within a few moments.

Ranbir lost colour when Inspector Jatin showed him his ID card. They walked to the drawing room and sat down on the sofa.

Ranbir nervously asked, "What can I do for you?"

Inspector Jatin began his interrogation without wasting any time.

"Where were you day before yesterday at night?"

"May I know the reason for your inquiry?"

"A blackmailer named Badshah was murdered day before yesterday night. After that, his Innova with his body was toppled over a cliff at Nalasopara. I got the report last evening and I went to his apartment at Kalina last night. I checked up his possessions at his apartment. He had sexually explicit photographs of Dr Sunanda and yourself." Jatin briefed.

"Yes, I had encountered Badshah, the blackmailer and I had paid ransom twice in the last ten months. Coming back to your first question, I was with my scriptwriter Varun day before yesterday night at his residence at Paidhuni. We were discussing the changes in the script of my film."

"Why did you pay the ransom instead of informing the police?"

"It was a question of our reputation and a lot of money was riding on my films."

"You are obviously main suspects for his murder," Jatin warned him.

"What! I have not committed any murder!" Ranbir tried to speak with a straight face. He tried to act shocked."

"How well do you know Veena?"

"You mean the CM's daughter? I have signed her as the heroine of my new film a few days back."

"She was also being blackmailed by Badshah. She is the other main suspect. I think you two teamed up to murder him. He was murdered by a Wesson pistol. I believe she has a pistol of the same make."

"I don't think Veena could have committed the murder."

"You can call up Veena and fix up an appointment in two hours. I will be a surprise visitor for her."

Ranbir could gather that it was a veiled order. He replied, "Okay, I will fix up a meeting at Volga restaurant at Churchgate at ten tonight!"

He called her up and fixed the meeting and walked with the inspector towards his parked Scorpio. They sat in the MUV and left.

Veena was waiting at the appointed time when both walked into the restaurant together.

Jatin asked Ranbir to take the seat next to her and he sat on the opposite side. She was worried to find a surprise visitor with Ranbir.

Ranbir ordered coffee for all of them. When the coffee was served and the waiter had moved away, they started the discussion.

"I am Inspector Jatin from the CID and I am investigating the murder of a drug dealer and blackmailer named Badshah, who was murdered day before yesterday and then his dead body with his Innova were thrown off a hill. I have learnt that he was blackmailing you and in the past he had blackmailed Ranbir twice. Did you murder him?"

"How could you level this allegation against me?" She pretended to look shocked.

"The ballistic report of the murder details that three bullets which had killed him were from a Wesson .38 caliber pistol. You have a licensed Wesson .38 caliber pistol."

"You are making false accusations and dragging my name into the mud. I can sue you for defamation." She countered defiantly.

Ranbir was impressed with Veena's guts.

Jatin slipped out four of her photographs in an envelope towards her.

Veena discreetly looked at the photographs and defended herself, "First, they are photo-shopped and you are maligning my image. Secondly, there could be hundreds of Wesson pistols in India. Moreover, I had lost my pistol about a month back."

Jatin knew that Badshah had photoshopped the pictures, so he paraphrased his allegation.

"You mean the man's face was not visible in any of the photographs. In some other photographs, which are still there in his computer, Badshah's face was visible. I have not brought those because he had blackmailed you with these photographs. You have murdered him with Ranbir's help because he had blackmailed him in the past too. And anyway, why did you not report the loss of your pistol to the police?"

"Why should I have felt threatened? He was my boyfriend. I could not even think of murdering him. And I forgot to lodge the complaint about my pistol," Veena said with a straight face.

Jatin asked her the last question, "Where were you that night?"

Veena replied, "I was with my Dad. We watched the documentaries made by Ranbir and we discussed the problems of water, power and air pollution in Maharashtra. After that we had dinner together."

"This is an open and a shut case of your teaming together and taking revenge. We have enough proof to nail the two of you," Jatin got tougher.

Veena showed a helpless expression and moved her hands up in despair, "You may assume whatever you want, but we have not committed the murder!"

Jatin was quite impressed with her cool reaction. He understood that it would be difficult to prove charges against her in the court because of the lack of solid evidence. He was sure that if he persisted to expose her, she would retaliate.

Ranbir had admitted that twice in the past he had paid money to the blackmailer. Therefore it went against his grain to murder a tough hard core criminal.

Jatin considered that Badshah had not generated any public sympathy as he was a thug. The police had not found any murder weapon and the case had been almost closed.

Jatin checked, "Can I pay the bill?"

Ranbir replied, "No, it's fine. I will pay!"

Jatin got up and said, "Fine my preliminary investigations are over. I do not want to ask you any further questions now."

Ranbir mentioned, "I will take a cab home."

Jatin accepted Ranbir's suggestion and he left them together at the restaurant and walked out alone.

"I have the power to stop the police inquiry but for that I would have to discuss the matter with my Dad," Veena said.

"The main incriminating articles are our photographs, the ballistic report about the bullets from Wesson pistol and my brief case containing cash," Ranbir said.

"As far as the pistol is concerned, I have already mentioned that it was lost about a month back. They will not be able to do anything about it. You have accepted that you had paid the ransom twice against your photographs; therefore you can't be considered to have had a motive. They can connect my photographs with the motive but I have admitted that he was my boyfriend. Therefore we are only suspects and they cannot stick a murder charge without solid evidence. Similarly, his enemies from the underworld, connected with his drug dealings could also be suspects."

"The police department would have to be extra careful about pressing the charges because if they cannot prove those, they would be faced with defamation charges to the tune of many crores and a few heads would definitely roll!"

Ranbir knew that she was powerful enough to put the police department on the mat.

6

Inspector Jatin called Ranbir and Veena and fixed a meeting for eleven in the morning at Volga restaurant. He sounded condescending during the telephonic discussions.

They assembled at the scheduled time.

Inspector Jatin tilted his head back and looked at both and conceded in a gentler tone, "I will not press any charges and I will also hand over all the photographs to you."

Veena responded on behalf of both of them, "For any dignified person, even a false charge of this proportion can be devastating. You have been reasonable, so we will reward you for your cooperation."

They fixed another meeting for the same evening at eight after Inspector Jatin had submitted his report in his office. In the report he summarized that Badshah, a drug dealer was killed when his Innova toppled over a hill at Nalasopara. The forensic report would point that he was under the affect of liquor while driving.

It was clear that the police would close the case because of the public apathy towards the drug dealer. In the evening, Inspector Jatin handed over a copy of the confidential report with his signature along with the photographs to Ranbir, Sunanda and Veena. In exchange, he was paid ten lakh rupees.

7

Ranbir drove for an hour and reached the meeting place. He noticed Veena seated over the stone railing. She wore an orange chiffon frock with flowers and white shoes.

The girl sitting by the sea had helped him immensely. She had provided him the access to eighty crores finance for his film and she had helped him get rid of the blackmailer and the police.

Ranbir had met a feisty girl for the first time in his life. All the while he had been besotted by Meera, but when he tried to get closer to her, she became unreachable. That had happened twice. He realized for the first time that he had been unnecessarily infatuated by Meera, whereas Veena was the right girl for him. He found Veena to be always accessible. She had never made him wait for her. On the other hand, Meera's moods varied with time. First she got lured by Karan's flamboyance and riches and second time she got tied by KJ's contract. Their relationship was never her first priority.

Veena spotted Ranbir and got down the stone railing to walk towards him.

"Hi", she greeted him.

"Hi, we had a terrific start to our friendship." He commented in high spirits, while he thought that she looked very charming.

They walked along the sea. On one side they had the panoramic view of the Arabian Sea, and on the other side, Hotel Taj stood in its majestic grandeur.

Veena was pleasantly surprised when Ranbir held her hand softly.

"You are a romantic person!" She chuckled.

"Why do you say that?" he asked with a playful smile.

"Do you have a special relationship with Meera?" She was coquettish.

Ranbir was taken aback because that very minute in his mind he was comparing her with Meera. He trusted that women had a sixth sense.

"We have a professional relationship only!" He tried to defend himself.

"The media doesn't seem to think so," she persisted.

"The media always exaggerates because that is their job!" he lied.

"What about your relationship with Sunanda?" She threw salvos.

"We both are good friends. She is happily married now," Ranbir said, surprised by Veena's inquisitiveness.

Veena looked convinced by his replies. She moved closer to him and lightly rested her head on his left shoulder. They looked into each other's eyes.

Ranbir rested his right hand on her nape and drew her face closer. They looked into each other's eyes and then they kissed.

"You are wonderful!" He complimented her.

"Why do you say that?" she asked.

"You have a winner's attitude."

"Thanks!"

"Let's do one thing. Let's go for a holiday to Goa!"

"It is a damn good idea. We can go on Friday morning."

Ranbir happily agreed and then both of them walked hand in hand to the Strand to watch *Inception*, the new science fiction film.

"I like Leonardo DiCaprio; he is so handsome! "

"It is the highest grossing film of the year!"

"What is the most important thing for you?"

"I want my film to win an international award."

After a pause he counter-questioned, "What about you?"

"For me, true love is most important," she replied.

Ranbir didn't believe her words, but he was touched. She was rich, powerful and attractive, and he wondered whether she understood the meaning of true love. He thought that probably it was her euphemism; she was most likely looking for something profound in her life.

"Do you get to spend time with your Dad?" he asked her.

"He is busy all the time, so I get very little time to spend with him. Initially I used to miss his company; ever since I have started working, I have also been busy."

She got gold class corner seats in the last row. He got two glasses of Pepsi and a large packet of popcorn from the counter. Both liked the film and came out of the theatre pretty impressed.

"I am submitting my resignation letter tomorrow. I think I will be relieved from duty by the end of the month. Then I can devote my full time to the film."

"I think we can start the shooting of the film in a month's time. By then, I will be free of the present workload."

They planned the trip to Goa, thinking it would be the perfect weekend getaway.

8

Ranbir and Veena took the early morning Indigo flight to Goa. The flight reached Dabolim Airport at ten in the morning. The airport was located at a very picturesque location near a beach lined with palm trees. The weather was very pleasant. They were picked up by a car sent by the Varca Beach Resort. The car dropped them to the club located at the beach in South Goa.

The resort was full of tourists and all of them were in a festive mood. He had booked a two bed room apartment. The wall to wall glass windows provided a panoramic view of the Arabian Sea. The walls and the tapestry were in ivory white.

They placed their suitcases on the stand in the ante room and lay down on the bed in the master bedroom to relax. Ranbir reached out and kissed Veena on her lips and she kissed him in return. Then she picked up the remote and switched on the TV.

They got attentive as soon as they saw the news on TV. The anchor had announced the breaking news. They saw Chief Minister Sudhakar Naik being interviewed as some protesters shouted slogans with placards in their hands. A sting operation in Vidharbha had revealed that one of State government MLAs had been caught taking a bribe of ninety lakh rupees. It was a direct allegation on his leadership and the opposition had geared up to attack the government in the forthcoming session in the parliament.

The CM was trying to defend himself in an interview by a press reporter. "I am sure these are fabricated charges by the opposition and we shall come out clean within a couple of days," CM said defending his government.

"The public will not be satisfied with a mere statement." The interviewer challenged him.

There were noisy scenes around and a big number of demonstrators, mostly from the opposition were shouting anti-government slogans.

Ranbir and Veena found that it was a recorded interview and the same news was being broadcasted at the other news channels also.

Veena made a call to her Dad on his personal mobile, but it was switched off. Then she called up his secretary in Mumbai to get information about him.

"Sir is quite upset due to the allegations, that's why he has switched off his mobile. He has been called by the high command in Delhi today at six. He is going by a special flight at three in the afternoon. I will let him know that you called as soon as I can contact him," the secretary replied.

Veena and Ranbir were also worried that in case the rumour blew up, it could lead to the cancellation of the grant for their film. They waited for a while in the hope that there would be a call from her Dad. Finally they made up their mind to take a flight back to Mumbai the same evening. They informed the reception that they would be checking out at two thirty and they wanted to be dropped to the airport for a 5 pm flight.

Veena said, "We will get the result by tonight. The high command in Delhi shall decide Dad's future."

"I hope everything will be okay."

"The opposition had been looking for arsenal to blast the government."

The next moment, her mobile rang. She was relieved to see that her Dad was on line and she talked to him affectionately, "Daddy, what is the problem? I am sorry but I can't be with you right now. I am in Goa on an assignment."

He replied, "I had talked with Sadashiv Patil, the Vidharbha MLA to admit to the press that he had accepted ninety lakhs as a loan for building a hospital and deny the bribe charges levelled against him. I have summoned by the high command in Delhi at six."

"Daddy, everything will be fine. I am sorry I am not with you in this moment of crisis."

"Do not worry; in politics such problems are common. At present the opposition has got the better of us."

She wished him good luck and then the line got disconnected.

The waiter had brought vegetable sandwiches and coffee. Ranbir signed the bill and tipped the waiter.

At around 2 pm, they freshened up and packed their belongings. They wheeled their suitcases to the reception. The same car had come to take them back to the airport.

Ranbir and Veena kept quiet for most of the time. They were waiting for the outcome of the meeting which was to be held between the high command and her Daddy.

"When we thought that all our hurdles had been cleared, this unexpected incident has happened," she said.

He looked towards her somberly, acknowledging her concern.

They were back in Mumbai at 6.30. She promised him that she would keep him abreast with the developments. They bade each other goodbye and took cabs back to their respective homes.

9

The high command made certain changes in the ministry. The Chief Minister was replaced to salvage the image of the party. On the next day in the legislative assembly, the governor gave oath to the new chief minister.

The new CM immediately ordered an inquiry to investigate the charges against the corrupt MLA. The damage control had been done. The public was satisfied with the changes, and for the party, the storm had blown over.

Sudhakar called Ranbir up. "You are aware that I do not hold power now. I had granted the sanction for your film due to my position. The new CM will reverse my decision in a few days. I am informing you in advance that you have to look for new sources to fund the film. You are not bound to take Veena as the heroine of the film. I am sorry for the inconvenience caused to you."

Ranbir replied, "Thanks for calling me and I am sorry for the problems you are facing. I will put my film on hold and I want to affirm that whenever I am able to resume the production of my film, Veena will be the heroine. I also wanted to check with you whether there will be problems in my getting the final payment for the documentaries."

"You will get the payment as per the contract because that payment is not huge and the work is almost complete."

Ranbir was once again in the dumps after hearing the news. He felt dejected and did not fancy the idea of venture capital.

He resolved to inform his staff that he had shelved the project indefinitely and that they would lose their jobs. For compensation, they would get one month's salary.

10

Ranbir was at home watching the clips from *Noora*. He was sure that the storyline was good and the film had very good potential. He thought the film could have been a work of art.

He thought about all the possibilities, including going in for the venture capital, which under the circumstances seemed too risky. Going in for the venture capital and subsequent public issue would mean handling too many imponderables. He finally decided to drop the project due to paucity of finance.

Ranbir had not felt so dejected on losing two beautiful women and his personal inheritance as he did on dropping his favourite project. While he was immersed in such pensive thoughts, he received Veena's call.

"Hey, I learnt from Daddy that the new CM will scrap the sanction of eighty crores which was promised to you. I know it is a big blow, but we will find a solution. Let us meet for lunch." She sounded optimistic.

He was impressed at her never-give-up attitude. Although he had decided to drop the project and to convey his decision to his team, he thought that there was no harm in discussing the matter with her for one last time.

He had a glimmer of hope after receiving her call.

Trattoria was a bright and colourful Italian restaurant and Veena had already seated herself at one of the tables in the middle of the hall.

"Madam, you are really punctual, I like your spirit," Ranbir complimented her with a smile.

"Thank you and the same goes for you!" she replied with a bright smile.

They ordered Italian Chianti red wine and grilled sea food.

"As you know the problem, I would suggest that you tell me what you think first," Ranbir said coming to the topic.

"OK, I learnt that the sanction of eighty crores from The Information and Broadcasting Ministry shall be dropped within a day or two. We have to find an alternative source of finance." She summed up.

"I will get fifty lakhs for the documentaries." Ranbir appraised her about his existing financial position.

"I can manage to contribute fifty lakhs from my sources." Veena generously offered from her side.

"Thanks for the offer, but I cannot accept any finance from you. Anyway, our total requirement is for about seventy crores," Ranbir mentioned.

"Now you needn't give me the female lead role under the changed circumstances." Veena butted in with a sulky expression.

Ranbir saw the situation getting out of hand, so he relented.

He looked into her eyes, lifted her chin with his right hand and cajoled her, "You are best suited for the role. Our problem is finance; let us focus only on that. I will accept your contribution, but we still need sixty-nine crores."

Veena smiled and suggested, "Why don't we ask Meera to ask KJ to finance our film?"

"Why would KJ finance our film? He is my rival."

"Meera is the female lead of his upcoming film *Meherbaan*, but she can pitch for you. KJ also makes films of the same genre. Your film can be made under his banner while you still remain the director. He will also gain by the collaboration."

"Your idea is farfetched and not so appealing because when the film gets released, his banner will hog all the credit and my name will not figure anywhere."

"What we can do is use Meera's influence to get an appointment with KJ to discuss the terms. He might agree to give you credit for the direction. Strangers can be bedfellows in business."

"I doubt if he'll be so accommodating."

"You have got the national award for direction. KJ will want a director of your caliber to work under his banner."

"OK, you call up Meera and request her for a joint meeting with KJ."

She looked hopeful as she picked up her purse and gestured towards the waiter to get the bill.

He also concluded that there was no harm in trying to find all possible solutions to end the embargo.

11

Meera enjoyed meeting her friends, who were just handful and they met sparingly. She had decided to always accept a good proposal. She had been busy with her shooting schedules for the film *Meherbaan* and modelling assignments. Sunanda was tied up after getting married and they hardly met. Veena was busy with her journalistic career. Her relationship with Ranbir wasn't the same as before. She was close to KJ, but he being a married man, maintained a cool distance in public. Radha, who worked for *Cosmopolitan* magazine was a nice girl, but they were not so close.

Meera and Veena met at the JW Marriot lobby as per the appointment. They walked with quick strides and hugged each other. They walked hand in hand to Reflections, the restaurant, and occupied a corner table. Veena got down to business after the initial exchange of pleasantaries.

"You know, Daddy had a setback and had to step down from his position. Consequently, Ranbir's sanction of eighty crores also got thwarted. I am also part of the project, so I am helping him find an alternative source of finance. You know that he cannot get the finance from the trade because his film is not a commercial film in the normal parlance. Can KJ be persuaded to make this film under his banner with Ranbir as the director?"

Meera thought over the proposal. She had referred Ranbir's name to Veena in the past and that is how he had got the documentaries. Ravi, the music director of Ranbir's film had referred her name to KJ and consequently she had got the lead role in his film *Meherbaan*. Ranbir, Veena and herself had a mutual give and take arrangement between them.

Meera gave serious thought to Veena's proposal and tried to understand its implications. Finally she inquired. "Ranbir must have considered the fact that in case *Noora* gets produced under KJ's banner, he would not get the credit."

"Ranbir wants to get the credit for directing *Noora* and he is fine with not getting the credit for producing the film. Probably these terms can be discussed in a joint meeting between them."

Meera felt a pang of jealousy; she could guess that the chit of the girl was close to Ranbir's heart.

She kept a straight face and replied, "I will present your proposal to KJ and shall call you up tomorrow."

They began to talk of other matters.

"What is new in the political scene?"

"Keep it to yourself. In the next party meeting, the High Command is likely to appoint Daddy as the Minister of Tourism at the Centre."

"Do you think there will be protests from the public or the opposition?"

"Public memory is short; moreover the scandal had its effect only up to state level politics. The government and the opposition have fixed a deal backstage and the noise makers are acquiescent."

"How does KJ work as a producer? Does he come to the sets on the shootings?" Veena asked.

"KJ's company is like a factory. He is more like a businessman than an artist. He is rarely on the sets. He has got assistant directors for each film. Abbas is the assistant director for my film. He is a fifty-year-old veteran and believes in big sets and outdoor shootings. We have been to New Zealand and Switzerland."

"So you are enjoying yourself?"

"Yes and no. I think there is more to learn in Ranbir's films. His way of working is very professional, because he experiments with new methods. You are very lucky that way!"

"I have got the break of my life, but unfortunately, the finance has become a hurdle."

After they finished their lunch, Veena paid the bill. Meera thanked her and they left the restaurant.

"I shall call you up tomorrow," Meera said before they parted.

KJ treated Meera in a special way. She was hopeful when she spoke to him about Ranbir's proposal. However, to her surprise, he didn't show much interest in making an offbeat film. He was so engrossed into mass production that he had stopped thinking about producing quality films.

Meera in her heart was disappointed with KJ's policy but was unable to do much. Her own career depended on his film *Meherbaan*. She realized that KJ was a businessman and his goal was only to get wealthier. For him, films didn't mean an expression of art, they were only a means to grow his wealth. She thought there was nothing wrong in that except that he was not paying his taxes honestly and his regular staff was underpaid.

She conveyed the message to Veena, "I am sorry but KJ doesn't wish to put his money on an offbeat film and is averse to taking such a risk."

"Thanks for making the effort." She answered her politely, without giving away her disappointment.

12

Veena received Meera's call when she was dressing up in the morning. She switched off the phone and gave vent to her disappointment by swearing loudly. Big tears rolled down her cheeks. She had not felt so helpless in a long time. She cried for a while and when she felt lighter, she washed her face and applied light make up. She decided to have tea in the garden so that she'd feel better.

Veena and her Dad had shifted to their own bungalow at Cuffe Parade. The bungalow had a big garden. In the garden, magnolias, chrysanthemums, gladiolus, roses and sunflowers bloomed. It also had four cane arm chairs and a wooden table laid there. She asked the servant to get tea and some biscuits. To her surprise, her Daddy joined her while she was sipping her tea.

"My lovely daughter, mind if I join you? I haven't had the pleasure of your company for quite some time. I wonder whether we live in the same house!" Her Dad said with a smile and sat down next to her. The helper brought a cup of tea for him too.

She was overwhelmed by his affection and her helplessness to solve her problem.

"What happened, who dare hurt my darling?"

"Daddy, the finance for the film has become an obstacle. I think Ranbir will have to drop the project."

"I know how much you both want this project. You don't worry; I will finance the film from my own resources. You can inform Ranbir to go ahead with his project."

She got up and garlanded her Daddy with both her arms. She quietly whispered in his ears, "Thanks Daddy, I love you!"

He also held her shoulders and responded smilingly, "I love you, my little one!"

He gave her the good news that the high command had formally conveyed to him that he would be appointed as the Minister of Tourism at the Centre. The next day paper would carry the news about the reshuffle in the cabinet ministry and he would be sworn in by the President the coming Monday.

She was happy with the change of tide. She was anxious to convey the good news about her Daddy financing the project to Ranbir.

Her mood had been transformed from sadness to joy. Father and daughter drank their tea over light-hearted banter. Both were at ease.

Her father finally got up, patted her on the back and excused himself. He had to attend a meeting.

She also got up and went to her room to make the phone call.

"Ranbir, our financial problem has been solved. Daddy has agreed to provide the finance from his personal resources." She happily announced.

"Thanks very much Veena, I am obliged to you and your dad." Ranbir warmly responded.

He further said, "The storm has finally blown over and now the time has come for us to implement the project."

They exchanged good wishes and disconnected the line.

13

Sudhakar had a meeting with Ranbir in Veena's presence.

"I have a lot of confidence in your ability to produce a quality film. I have funds available and I thought it best to invest in your film. I understand your total requirement is eighty crores. The cash flow will be suited to your requirement." He said magnanimously.

"I am thankful to you for your offer," Ranbir replied with a smile.

Veena was also beaming with joy and she held her Dad's hand to express her gratitude.

The meeting got over and Ranbir left for his office to send letters to his team members telling them that they'd restart the project. He couriered the letters and left for his home.

On his way back, he was surprised to receive a call from Inspector Jatin.

He had called up for a meeting with him and Veena. He had mentioned that he had some special news for them.

They assembled at Ranbir's apartment over a cup of tea the same evening.

Inspector Jatin said, "You have an enemy in the film world."

Veena looked at Jatin with a surprised look.

Ranbir uttered, "You mean KJ?"

Veena was shocked to hear Ranbir's guess.

Jatin looked at them and said, "Yes, last time I had concealed some information about him. I had got two more photographs from Badshah's computer. He took out hard copies of the two photographs from his front pocket and placed before them. They saw that in the first photograph, Badshah was holding the CCTV camera and KJ was sitting next to him and in the second photograph Badshah was receiving a few bundles of currency from KJ.

Jatin looked at Ranbir and said, "KJ had been scheming to tarnish your image. He recruited Badshah from the underworld to snoop into your private life. He gave him the CCTV camera and paid him a hefty amount and helped him get entry into Sunanda's Delhi hotel room. But Badshah got smarter and lied to KJ that he didn't manage to get any scandalous pictures. He, without KJ's knowledge, blackmailed you. After eight months, KJ once again recruited him to get your scandalous pictures."

Jatin looked towards Veena and said, "KJ also tipped him about you being the new heroine of Ranbir's new film. Badshah was successful in seducing you and he took some scandalous photographs to blackmail you."

Veena successfully hid her reaction by looking aghast.

Jatin swept a look at both of them and continued, "KJ somehow learnt that in the past Badshah had deceptively changed his game plan. He learnt that he had not only laid hands on scandalous photographs in the past, but had gone further and collected the money from Ranbir and seduced Veena. KJ was shocked at his double game and got him knocked off. The police had wrongly concluded that he was eliminated by the drug mafia."

Ranbir and Veena were listening to Jatin with their eyes wide open.

Veena looked at Jatin and asked, "Will the police open the case again?"

"No. Neither the public nor the police have any sympathies for Badshah, but we know that KJ is a criminal and he will act maliciously against Ranbir in future as well."

Ranbir said, "I will be careful. Thanks very much for cautioning me!"

Jatin felt relaxed after the meeting was over. Veena remained quiet because he had believed that she and Ranbir were innocent.

Ranbir was forgiving by nature but Veena was vengeful. She could not let KJ go scot free. She resolved to punish him soon.

Chapter - VI

1

KJ had followed Badshah's Innova from his apartment at Kalina to Hotel Taj Lands End in his BMW X5. He saw him taking a U turn near the hotel and stopping his MUV on the other side of the road. He saw a Mercedes M parked on his side. He was surprised to see Ranbir getting out of the car holding a large briefcase and Badshah walking towards him with an envelope in his hand. When he saw Badshah exchanging the envelope with the briefcase, he knew that he had been conned by Badshah.

When Ranbir returned from his long trip from the villages of Maharashtra, KJ learnt through Meera that the Ministry of Information and Broadcasting was clearing eighty crores grant for Ranbir's film *Noora*. Moreover, Veena, the CM's daughter was replacing Meera as the heroine of the film. He had been stung with jealousy once again. He had seen Ranbir's meteoric rise from a nobody to a famous director of artistic films, which were also box office hits. Then he had engaged Badshah for the second time to dig out something scandalous about Ranbir and Veena that he could use against them.

KJ was convinced that Badshah had taken scandalous photographs in the first assignment also but he had not surrendered those photographs to him, and instead had used them to blackmail Ranbir directly for a larger amount.

KJ was seething with anger and he resolved to punish Badshah for his disloyalty. However, his main target was still Ranbir and as Badshah was blackmailing him, he decided that first he would let Badshah milk Ranbir.

To his shock, he got the news five days later that Badshah's charred body had been recovered from his burnt Innova at Nalasopara. KJ was convinced that Ranbir was behind the murder.

KJ put brakes on his own plans temporarily and decided to lie low. He was afraid that in the hunt for the murderers, the police would find some incriminating evidence against him too. Something that brought to light that he was responsible for setting up Badshah against Ranbir.

2

Meera was busy with *Meherbaan*. That was her fifth film in eight years in the film industry. She had already appeared in a number of advertisements and had been the brand ambassador of over four products in the past. Her fortune had grown steadily. But her schedules had become extremely hectic and she desired to finally hang up her boots after the completion of *Meherbaan*.

Meera contemplated that she would have to be much more disciplined being a megastar and she would have to sacrifice a great deal, starting with small things like giving up non vegetarian food, desserts, alcohol and cigarettes. She enjoyed these small pleasures of life and was not ready to make the sacrifice. She realistically assessed that she would not be able to become a mega-star because her best phase of filmdom was already behind her, so she decided to enjoy her life as much as possible.

KJ had been eyeing her for quite a while. Once he gathered the courage and asked her for a date. Meera was rather lonely so she agreed and invited him for dinner at her place.

Meera ordered main dishes from Fortune Select Exotica hotel and decorated her home with white gladiolas. She wore a white chiffon sari. When KJ arrived, she greeted him with a broad smile and made him comfortable in the drawing room. KJ wore a white Armani suit with black Gucci shoes.

On his arrival, he presented her with a diamond set. She was floored.

"How beautiful! I just love it." she exclaimed and kissed him on his cheek.

He remarked nonchalantly, "Oh, it is nothing!"

She poured two pegs of scotch and brought out the fish fingers and chicken tikkas for starters.

KJ knew how to be overindulgent. He had dreamt of this night for a long time. He had a wife, a son and two daughters at home. He was in his late forties, flabby, balding, and yet here he was, coveting a lead actor in her twenties. He believed in the power of money.

After two drinks they loosened up and he held her by the waist and drew her close towards him. She laughed and bent forward. He kissed her awkwardly.

"I don't want a one night stand," he uttered while trying to kiss her.

"What are your intentions?" she remarked playfully.

"I want to marry you!"

Meera laughed and asked him, "You are already married and have three teenaged children!"

KJ was serious and he replied, "You will be my second wife and I will provide you with an apartment at Juhu, luxury cars and we shall go on holidays to the best destinations in the world. When I am not working, I shall spend all my free time with you."

"That would be unfair to your wife and children," she said in a mellowed tone.

"I have provided them with all the comforts. They will manage well on their own. I love you and I want to be happy," KJ said seriously.

Meera had fallen in and out of love relationships. She thought that love was fleeting, which invariably left her in pain. She needed to be practical. She knew that as a heroine, her rating would decline with the passage of time. She was at the threshold of marriageable age and she could visualize that time was fast slipping by. She was presented with an opportunity of marrying a successful producer. She dreamt that she would have foreign jaunts to Italy and Spain. She would have imported cars and she would have a luxury apartment at Juhu. She also yearned for the love and care which KJ promised her.

She thought over the proposal and finally decided in favour of security rather than fleeting love. "Okay. I will to marry you!"

They happily had dinner and parted after a long kiss.

3

KJ did not think twice about how his wife would react. He had married twenty-two years back when he was a struggling producer. It was a culmination of his physical and social needs at that time. In the last two decades, his status had changed. He had been able to accumulate a good amount of wealth. He believed that he could buy anything with money. He believed that the needs of his family were more than met with.

In later years, he wished to hand over his film production unit to his son and marry off his two daughters to wealthy families. His wife was submissive and she spent most of her time engrossed in religious rituals. She had adjusted to be happy with her daughters, son and her religious activities.

In India, unless the first wife made a complaint of bigamy against the husband, the second marriage stood valid. In case the first wife simply never approached the court for justice, the fraudulent second marriage would stand strong. KJ had handed over their bungalow, gold, shares and cars to his wife, son and two daughters. He knew that as his family had more wealth than they'd ever require, they wouldn't complain.

KJ made quick arrangements and on the successive weekend in a private ceremony, in presence of a priest and two witnesses, he and Meera tied the knot.

The film fraternity was taken by surprise. But such marriages and liaisons were common in the glamour world. Meera was interviewed by some film magazines but the matter cooled off thereafter. Many of the old veterans in the film world like Hema Malini, Shabhana Azmi and Sri Devi had tied the knot with married men in their days.

Meera and KJ went to Venice and Spain for their honeymoon. On her return, she chose a five bedroom apartment on tenth floor of a high rise building facing Juhu beach. She had a clear view of the sea from both her drawing room and master bed room.

She decorated her home tastefully with Belgian furniture. She bought two swanky cars and engaged two servants and a driver. KJ spent almost all the evenings with her in her new apartment.

Meera knew that she had made compromises in her life, but had no regrets.

4

Ranbir was stunned with Meera's decision to marry KJ. He knew KJ's viciousness. He thought that as her close friend and past lover, it was his duty to warn her against KJ's criminal activities. Unfortunately, by then, it was too late.

Ranbir also realized that he had probably misunderstood her. He thought that she most likely knew about KJ's character but she had decided to overlook it because the material rewards were too great. Ranbir further considered the possibility that KJ could also be innocent and he might not have had any connection with Badshah's actions. It could be that Inspector Jatin had misinformed him and Veena against KJ, whereas Badshah had blackmailed both of them without his initiative. There was a possibility that the photographs in which KJ and Badshah were together could have meant something else, and not at Badshah being his agent.

Ranbir remembered the time he and Meera had spent together. There were nostalgic memories which he could not erase. He knew she had taken this decision in haste. He realized his financial vulnerability had been one of the reasons of their failed love. Even till date his financial situation was dicey and he knew that if his new film failed, he would be in a dire state.

However, her desertion didn't cause him the blues he had experienced in the past. He was in a way relaxed that his infatuation for her had weathered off. He realized that their love could never have survived the tests and tribulations of time.

In the last few years he had learnt to be less emotional and more analytical about his romances. He had learnt to open up after he was jilted. Consequently, he was less obsessive and valued dependable relationships. He was more focused on his job and social interactions. Sunanda, and later on Veena had filled the void created by Meera's absence. Veena was his rock and he realized that in her companionship, his true artistic qualities blossomed.

He had also managed his time better, and as a result, in one year, their film had almost been completed. He was happy that he hadn't had to deal with KJ for the finance for his film. He remembered the old maxim, "Everything happens for the better!" He thanked God for His blessings.

5

"What would you like to have?" The airhostess politely asked Ranbir. She had the trolley stacked with an assortment of liquors and beverages. She smiled and paused for his response.

Ranbir woke up from his dream and looked up. There was bright light coming through the windows and jetliner was cruising at 45,000 feet above the Atlantic. He saw a smiling French air hostess waiting for his response.

"Oh, what can you offer?"

"I have Black Label scotch, Guinness Draught beer, Portico Red wine, Smirnoff Vodka."

"I will have a scotch with soda and ice."

She poured him a large peg, dropped two cubes of ice, filled the glass with soda and handed him the drink. She also gave him a plate of Scottish cottage cheese.

He delightfully sipped his drink. He felt the smoothness of the drink on his palate. He looked at his watch, which he had set according to New York time. His flight had taken off from Paris about an hour back.

He looked outside the window. The sky was clear and he felt good looking at the beauty of nature. He picked up the Air France magazine and leafed through it.

The plane had a smooth landing at the John F. Kennedy International Airport. He went through customs and came to the exit.

"Taxi!"

A yellow Chevrolet sedan halted at the tarmac road. He pushed his suitcase and settled himself beside it.

"Hotel Victoria, 47, West Street!"

He called up his consultant to inform him about his arrival. "Mr. Shekhar, my flight has landed and I shall be at my hotel in thirty minutes. Will it be okay if we can meet at five in the evening?"

"Fine, I will meet you at five at the Piccadilly restaurant," his consultant replied.

He felt relaxed after the appointment was fixed. He looked at his watch and realised he had full five hours to himself.

Once he checked into the room, he called up Veena.

"Hey, I am in my hotel in New York. I am meeting my consultant in the evening."

"Well, call me up after the meeting. All the best!"

He freshened up and changed into his pyjamas. He wanted to relax for a while before getting ready for his meeting.

His mobile alarm woke him up at 3.00. He freshened himself and changed into a business suit. At 4.00, he picked up the DVD of the English version of *Noora* for the meeting.

At five, his consultant Shekhar walked in. They shook hands and then walked towards a corner table.

"New York is a nice city. I always look forward to my visits here," Ranbir began a polite conversation.

"Oh yes, the city is buzzing with life, though after 9/11, security across the city has been beefed up."

After a pause, Shekhar came to the main point. "Well, have you brought DVD of your film *Noora*?"

Ranbir handed Shekhar the DVD and a banker's cheque of one million USD towards the full consultancy payment and business expenses.

Shekhar gave an introduction about his expertise. "The international awards are given by Europe and the US based Academy of Motion Pictures for meritorious achievement in feature film making. The awards are given in twenty-four categories. The Academy does not disclose the names of its members. However, they claim to have over seven thousand members, who represent different areas of film making. Some of the members include Tom Hanks, Richard Gere, Jean Reno, Juliette Binoche, Claude Chabrol, Angelina Jolie, Madonna, Bryan Adams, Eric Clapton, Halle Barry, Wilbur Smith and Tim Burton."

"How do the nomination and voting processes take place?"

"Members from each of the areas vote to determine the nominees in their respective categories. All voting members are eligible to select the best picture nominees. The nomination ballots are then mailed in December to the screening committee and the final nominations are announced in January every year. The final nomination ballots are re-sent to members for voting where each member can vote," Shekhar replied.

"And what is the eligibility criterion?"

"A film has to be of feature length, over forty minutes and must open in the previous calendar year. It also has to be released in a commercial motion picture theatre in Los Angeles, London and Paris for at least a week each. I will make arrangements to release *Noora* in one theatre in London, one theatre in Los Angeles and one theatre in Paris next month. I will also arrange three private previews and meetings with three members of the Academy who are based in New York during the next four days. People have the impression that the best films get awards. In fact, so many films get produced in the world that it is impossible for the Academy members to even view them. There is a screening process but only those films can have the chance to win which are shown to the nomination committee. That is where the public relations and marketing come into play." Shekhar briefed him.

Ranbir was aware about Shekhar's experience and his level of high contacts in Hollywood and the European film community. Though Shekhar had no doubts about *Noora* being a top quality film, yet a number of preview screenings and a lot of promotion activities were needed to get his film nominated.

Shekhar had lined up for Ranbir a number of interviews along with private screenings with the members of the International Award Committee.

Ranbir had interviews and a private screenings with Michael Douglas, Halle Barry and Wilbur Smith in New York in the successive three days.

He flew to Los Angeles and had private screening for directors Steven Spielberg and Tim Burton.

Shekhar also organized a private screening for twenty more members of the International Award Committee in different places in Los Angeles and also arranged Ranbir's visits to Kodak Studio, MGM and Universal Films.

He flew to Mumbai after a sojourn of twelve days.

7

Ranbir had only a brief stay in India as Shekhar had lined up a few meetings with top directors and actors in various cities in France and a few preview screenings of *Noora* dubbed in French.

Later Shekhar had lined up a few screenings of *Noora* in English in London also.

Ranbir and Veena flew to France together. The Air France plane touched Charles de Gaulle Airport early in the morning.

France was an exquisite journey of discovery around every corner.

They had a meeting with Claude Chabrol in Lyon. Ranbir and Veena travelled the city together.

They explored the UNESCO World Heritage City of Lyon, a treasure house of museums and cathedrals. They walked on Saint George's footbridge and enjoyed the peaceful charm of the SaÔne river. It was a delightful experience to walk into the traditional Bouchon Bakery to discover why Lyon was called the French capital of gastronomy.

They met Jean Reno in Paris during his second stop.

They went to the Eiffel Tower, Moulin Rouge, and Montmartre – the places which made their imaginations run wild. There was still so much more to discover about Paris. The city of lights was full of places of delight.

The Louvre museums, Musée du Louvre were magnificent and needed no introduction. The Parisians sipped espressos outside restaurants and on terraces spread out on the pavements of the capital. They even managed to attend the famous Moulin Rouge show which was a beautiful reminder of the culture of French dance, drama and music.

Ranbir and Veena's next stop was Nice where they had meeting with Juliette Binoche at Monte Carlo.

The meeting went well and they toured Monte Carlo, Nice, Monaco, Cannes and St. Paul. Each day brought some new experiences, which showed them new facets of life.

The day before they were leaving Nice for Bordeaux, they met Emanuelle at the reception of Best Western Alba Hotel. She was from a small island in the Indian Ocean and she worked as a receptionist there. She asked him about his experience in the bus on the Tour de Nice. She also showed a keen desire to visit India. They exchanged their email addresses. They asked her if they could go to watch a film in Nice. She directed them to a theatre named Mercury at Garibaldi.

It was easy to catch a train from Avenue de Medicine and Garibaldi was only four stops away.

In a few minutes they could locate the theatre. The booking clerk informed them that there was an English film named *Harvey Milk* after about twenty minutes. The film had been nominated for eight Oscars. It was about a movement in San Francisco, USA in the 1970s about the civil rights of homosexuals. Harvey Milk – who was the representative of the homosexuals and was elected as the senator – was murdered in 1978. Harvey knew that by heading the movement, he had put his life in danger. In case of his unnatural death, for posterity, he had put complete sequence since the birth of the movement till his last day, in a tape.

The next stop was Bordeaux. They had a meeting with Catherine Deneuve there.

They remembered Bordeaux for vineyards, distilleries and wine tasting. They were offered the best wines to taste at wine museum and a distillery in the suburbs of Bordeaux.

They were in the last lap of their tour. They were comfortably seated in the TGV, which took them from Bordeaux to Paris. They reached the airport by afternoon.

Ranbir and Veena had different plans from there onward. Veena had to catch her flight to London and Ranbir had to catch his flight to Mumbai. Veena had a few preview screenings scheduled in London for a few members of International Award Nomination Committee.

They were well in time for the Air France flight from Paris to London and Paris to Mumbai. They kissed and parted there.

At that time the next day, Ranbir would be busy in promotional activities. He had mixed feelings, which he supposed was normal at such a time. After almost thirteen days of travelling, sightseeing and meeting people from France, he would be home to his office staff and his team.

8

In a couple of days, Veena also returned from London.

In India *Noora* had got undue publicity; it had been banned in Maharashtra. It was condemned on the charges of obscenity.

Around the same time, *Noora* was shown in one theatre in London, one theatre in Paris and one theatre in LA County for a week each. The film was acclaimed as an artistic film and it got nominated for the International Award by the Ijury.

Ranbir received the award as the Best Director for the feature film. The award was presented in a glittering show in Los Angeles in February and it was telecast live worldwide. Ranbir and Veena were special invitees. Ironically, the same film which was banned in Maharashtra, was being appreciated as a work of art by the international community. They had the impression that though Bollywood produced more films than Hollywood, yet the quality of the films was inferior and they were labelled as too loud and unrealistic. *Noora* brought a change in their perception. They welcomed the film for its simplicity and realism. After a long gap of five decades, the potential of Indian Cinema was a force to be reckoned with.

9

Ranbir was being interviewed by BBC interviewer, Minal on 92.3 FM channel.

"How would you rate yourself on a scale of 1 to 10 as a director?"

"I think I will rate myself at 5."

"How will you rate Satyajit Ray?"

"I will rate him at 7."

"How will you rate Danny Boyle?"

"I will rate him at 5."

"What is the reason that you have rated Satyajit Ray higher than both yourself and Danny Boyle?"

"In my mind, a story should be simple and close to reality. In this respect, Satyajit Ray in his debut film *Pather Panchali* had presented a far more credible story about the bond between a brother and sister in a village in India. Danny Boyle had made his film, *Slumdog Millionaire* with an almost incredible plot where a slum boy becomes a millionaire through a TV game show. My story is about a small town girl who faces failure in her personal life but comes out extremely successful as a social reformer."

"What are your plans hereafter?"

"I am keen on creating remakes of some classics. I am also interested in making films for international community to project India in its true glory!"

"On behalf of all the listeners and your fans, I wish you a lot of success for your film *Noora* and for your future plans."

Two films were launched on the same day. They were not of the same genre but the hoopla surrounding their releases was unprecedented.

The first was Ranbir's artistic *Noora*. Veena was launched as the heroine. It was released in both Hindi and English languages.

The second was KJ's commercial film *Meherbaan,* with Meera as the heroine.

Veena was being touted as Ranbir's current flame. Meera was being touted as Ranbir's ex flame and KJ's new catch.

Ranbir did not want to have the image of a womanizer but as the buzz was fueling the publicity of his film, he took it in his stride.

Noora had been released in forty countries in Hindi, English and French. At the same time the ban in Maharashtra had been lifted due to public protests. So the film was released all over India as well.

Both sides had splurged huge amounts on advertising. These launches were just before Holi, when people all over India were in a festive mood.

10

The journalist from NDTV for the program *Filmy Khabaren* interviewed Ranbir.

"What is the theme of your film?"

"Noora is the name of the heroine of the film. She is the daughter of an Indian Army officer, who got paralyzed in the Kargil war. She is very proud of her father and helps him to lead a spirited life despite his being handicapped.

"Noora and her father live in a bungalow at Leh. She meets a young businessman from Pune, who had come to Leh on a holiday. They fall in love. He proposes marriage to her. She agrees but puts a condition that he would have to look after her father. He was not strong enough to take up the responsibility and he backs out. She is heartbroken and she resolves that she will never marry.

"She starts working towards a few eco projects on drip irrigation and water recycling. She puts in a lot of effort but a rich man who had financed the project takes away all the credit for the good work done by her.

"She has to struggle through life. After a few years her father dies. She is alone and by then in her thirties. She decides to migrate to Gurgaon. She buys an apartment and starts offering her experience in the field of water conservation. Her projects get a lot of success. She adds her expertise in diverse fields like solar heating and bio plants. She also starts cooperatives for women, where native skills of women get channelized in making handicrafts. She gets accolades for her good work. She becomes a well-known social worker. She also gets nominated to the Rajya Sabha."

"Your film is like a documentary. Why will the aam aadmi go to watch your film?"

"They will like the film because of the strong character of a woman who wins against all odds."

"You have made artistic commercial films in the past as well. What inspired you to risk so much of capital on a film with a social angle?"

"I want my film to be viewed in India as well as abroad."

The film had very good ratings from the media and it did well in all the circuits. The film crossed a revenue of around a hundred crores in the first week itself.

KJ was also interviewed.

He narrated, "Meherbaan is an action film about vendetta. The hero has been victimized by the villain. In the process, the hero meets the heroine and they fall in love. The villain creates serious problems for both. In the end the hero defeats the villain. The film has fight scenes, dances and shots taken in a number of gorgeous foreign locations."

People had got tired of seeing so many vendetta films with the result that *Meherbaan* flopped after a week's run. For the first time, KJ lost money on a film.

In Mumbai, a film producer's market value is rated by the performance of his last film. *Meherbaan's* poor results triggered a kind of chain reaction for KJ's films in the pipeline. Consequently, the financers became cautious and they started demanding refund of their loans. In three months' time, KJ either had to sell some assets or he had to stop his production unit. He had sunk in over one hundred crores in three films which were in the pipeline. He was on the hot seat. The initial casualties of the crisis were his office at Bandra and his studio at Andheri East. He had to sell these two assets to raise eighty crores.

KJ's infatuation with Meera had also evaporated because he had spent over twenty crores on her. In the past he had been ecstatic in her company, but later he felt burdened by her presence. He decided to separate from her.

KJ was shrewd and had not passed on the ownership of Meera's apartment to her. Meera had the property documents lying around for one year. She could notice a change in KJ's attitude after *Meherbaan* flopped at the box office. She understood that something was amiss. His visits had become few and far between.

KJ asked her to give him the property documents. He casually mentioned that he wanted the documents for the official transference to her name. She trusted him and handed him the set. To her shock, seven days later, she got a call from Sapra, a dubious property agent. He made a veiled threat to her that she had to vacate the apartment in three days' time as the property had already been sold to his client. She was shocked to learn that KJ had decieved her. That was the first time that she consulted a lawyer about the eviction threat from the property agent and also about her legal status as his second wife. She was informed that she could fight for her rights and she could get compensation on both the counts from the court, but as it was a civil case, the matter could drag on for years. She knew that KJ was a devious person and he could manipulate the legal battle and frustrate her by getting the trial dates postponed. She realized her mistake. She swore to herself that she would never forgive him for his treachery and decided to cut him off from her life. She vacated the apartment and left behind the furnishings as well as the two cars. She moved out with only her personal belongings.

KJ sold the apartment along with the two cars for eighteen crores.

Meera contemplated her two failed relationships. In both cases, she had been left high and dry by her partners. However, between her two partners, she didn't bear as much malice towards Karan as she did towards KJ. She considered that Karan was plain stupid but KJ was a devious man. She felt deeply hurt due to the personal humiliation she had endured.

She moved back to her original apartment at Palm Beach Road in Navi Mumbai which she had kept locked after her marriage.

She applied for a divorce on the grounds of mutual consent. The divorce was granted to her in six months' time.

She decided to take a break. She had been through a bad phase. The memories of her failed relationship were still haunting her. She decided to go to London.

11

Meera reached Covent Garden, London. The Christmas decorations had been completed and the place looked colourful. There were a lot people in and around. They had come to shop, eat and enjoy the festivities.

She was approached by a girl in early twenties, with Asian features.

"Hello, my name is Aliya and I am from Lahore, Pakistan. We are on a mission here; can I talk to you for a few minutes?"

Meera hesitated but as she found her attractive and educated, she accepted her proposal. They seated themselves on a nearby bench. There was an atmosphere of fun and gaiety.

"I belong to Pakistan and you belong to India; though the relations between our two countries are unfriendly, yet we have so much in common – we have similar features, we speak similar languages and we have the same cultural back ground. Women in both our countries should get more freedom." Aliya tried to create a bond between the two.

Meera amicably replied, "I agree with you. There is more freedom for women in India than in Pakistan, yet a lot needs to be done. Generally they are perceived as the weaker sex in both the countries and their status needs to be uplifted."

Meera found Aliya to be trustworthy and they became quite close while talking. Aliya invited Meera to her apartment and she agreed. Both of them took a cab to reach Aliya's house near the Charring Cross Road station.

Aliya's apartment had been decorated tastefully. She had a big picture of Kim Kardashian on the wall.

Aliya offered a glass of scotch to Meera. They sat down on the bed and sipped their drinks.

"Aliya, what do you do?" Meera asked her after some casual conversation about London and how different life here was as against in India and Pakistan.

"I am a student of political science. I am a member of the group named Reach Out. We have members from India, Pakistan, Bangladesh and Sri Lanka. Our head office is in London."

"What do you guys do?"

"Our goal is to upgrade the status of women. Women should be treated as individuals. Every family should provide equal opportunities to a girl child."

Meera asked further, "How do you work towards your goal?"

"We try to bring that change in our society. We educate through staging plays."

"In what way can I contribute?"

"As you are an actor, you could do that job very effectively."

"Where do you stage your plays? I am based in Mumbai. In case you plan to enact plays there, I want to participate."

"Our plays have been staged in small towns in all four countries. We have had forty-five shows till date. We will try staging a play in Mumbai soon."

Meera felt highly sensitized about the problems of women in a male-dominated society. She had herself been ill treated by various men. She was moved by Aliya's passion. She thought that Reach Out was doing a commendable job. She took out ten fifty-pound notes from her purse and gave a donation to the organization.

After a cup of coffee, they moved out. She got into a cab and then both waved each other goodbye.

12

Meera had enjoyed her trip to London fully.

Her KLM flight took off in the morning. The airplane was flying above the clouds. The morning light was filtering through the windows. She was in the executive class and there were only six passengers other than her. Two flight attendants served them morning tea and coffee.

She took the stock of her assets. She had a large beach apartment, ten crores in liquid assets, a car and an MUV. She had gold and diamond jewellery valued around a crore and stocks in a few blue chip companies valued around two crores.

She was twenty-nine and independent. She had a lot of acquaintances but not many friends. She wanted to take corrective steps regarding major decisions of her life.

She had taken the first corrective action of divorcing KJ.

The second corrective action needed was about her career. After the failure of *Meherbaan*, she was offered character roles. Though in commercial cinema there was not much scope for acting for women, yet she could still get some character roles and some modelling assignments. The offered amounts for the character roles were far less than what she had commanded as a lead actor, therefore the whole idea of continuing her film career was not very attractive to her.

She decided to take up social work. She was confident about her managerial abilities. She thought that she would be able to utilize her knowledge, which she had acquired as a student of social sciences at IP College. She thanked god that she had never had any problems regarding money so far. She thought it was the opportune time to give back to the society.

When Bill Gates had come to India, she had attended one of his meetings at the Taj. She was highly motivated when he had asked rich people to donate half of their wealth to the poor. She knew that many industrialists like Azim Premji, Dr Narayan Murthy and Ratan Tata were doing a commendable job for helping the poor in India. However, their contribution was still very meager when faced with the varied problems of a vast country. She had the choice to keep herself aloof from the problems of the poor and carry on with her affluent lifestyle, but she decided to choose the difficult path. She decided to rise above the level of mere existence and to do whatever was within her power to help the needy.

She thought she could enlist a few more persons with her to form an organization. She would make her mother the chairperson and would get two professionals from the industry.

It was quite a challenge to do something worthwhile for the society. She also realized that such thoughts occurred to her mostly when she was travelling. When she was at home or when she was working, she was involved in day to day activities. She didn't think much beyond herself or her work at that time. When she was in familiar surroundings, she couldn't see the bigger picture, but when she travelled, the world opened up with various possibilities.

The other reason was that during the past seven months, she had been absolutely alone and she had time for introspection. In a way, bad experiences had been a blessing in disguise for her. She had learnt from her mistakes.

Meera knew that the time had come to bring a change. Victor Hugo had written, "No one can resist an idea whose time has come." All this time, she had thought about herself. That was fine as she had the potential to make it in the celluloid world and that gave her the leverage to do something for the less fortunate.

The flight landed at Chhatrapati Shivaji International Airport at 5.00 pm. Under normal circumstances, she would have felt low in going back home alone, especially after a holiday. But this time, she had resolved to achieve something worthwhile. She was happy after having rediscovered herself.

13

Meera had chartered upon a new journey. She had a clear goal in her mind. She planned of creating a fund of rupees two hundred crores to offer scholarships to deserving students in the field of Information Technology. She possessed seed capital and she worked towards attracting major funds from the industry. She decided to tie up with all IT institutes in three cities – Pune, Bangalore and Hyderabad.

Meera purchased an office at Vashi. She named her social organization, Ujagar and she got Mr Vijay Mehta and Mrs Malti Bhatnagar, two professionals to lead the organization. Both the professionals had good backgrounds. Mr Mehta was seventy-six and Mrs Malti Bhatnagar was fifty-nine years old. While Mehta had worked with Asia South Pacific Association dealing with basic and adult education, Malti had worked as a project officer in United Nations Development Fund for Women and she had good project management experience.

Meera along with Vijay and Malti prepared the memorandum of association and got the organization, Ujagar registered. They announced scholarships for two students from two IT institutes in each of three cities.

They gradually showcased their efforts in the form of a short film and sent the DVDs of the film to heads of fifty top industries.

The response was encouraging. Meera was granted interviews with Ratan Tata, Dr Narayan Murthy, Azim Premji, Adi Godrej, Kiran Mazumdar and many more. She raised two hundred and ten crores in a period of six months.

She made a permanent endowment in two good IT institutes in each of the three cities so that each year at least thirty deserving students from economically weaker sections could get scholarships for further studies.

14

Veena was one of the new breed of fitness freaks. She spent almost two hours each day at the gym. The gym was on two floors and she would run up the stairs twenty times each way. She would then begin pectoral, weights and the treadmill. The exercises kept her body well-toned.

She was confident that she had the power to carve her destiny. She had acquired this trait from her Dad.

It was midnight when Veena dressed herself in black tight rubber top and stretch pants, rubber shoes and a mask. She started her Vento and drove to a bungalow at Juhu. She parked her car at the bend; she got off and walked parallel to the boundary wall for ten meters. She jumped over the boundary wall and hid herself behind the bushes. Once she was sure nobody had noticed her entry, she swiftly moved towards the two storey building. She noticed two guards with rifles, one near the gate and the other at the porch. She deftly climbed over the pole and then on the parapet. She had moved stealthily in the darkness. She peeped from behind the curtain into the bedroom. She saw KJ sitting on his chair with a glass of whiskey on the table. He was brooding about something.

Veena swiftly jumped inside the room and pulled out her Wesson pistol, pointing it at him.

KJ was shocked and his face was drained of all the blood.

She warned him in a stern tone, "Don't move or raise your voice, otherwise I will shoot!"

She moved swiftly and closed the exit door.

He asked in a low voice, "Who are you?"

She removed her mask and said, "I am Veena. You had paid Badshah to take scandalous photographs to ruin my reputation."

"I don't know what you're talking about. Who Badshah? I am innocent!" He denied the charge.

"You wanted to tarnish Ranbir's image as well."

"No, I have never done anything. Ranbir and I have healthy competition."

She rubbished him and placed two photographs of him with Badshah.

He looked at the photographs and looked aghast.

He begged, "I have lost a fortune. My film *Meherbaan* has lost a lot of money. My career is in ruins. Please have mercy on me!"

She pointed her pistol against him and questioned, "You had sent a hardened criminal against me and Ranbir. You wanted to defame us. On what ground should I offer you mercy?"

He begged, "I have a family to look after...a wife, a son and two daughters."

She stated sternly, "You had no conscience when you acted towards ruining our careers and reputations."

KJ looked defeated.

Veena finally warned, "I am sparing your life, but if you try any tricks in the future, then I will not spare you."

She slipped the Wesson pistol back in her pocket and stealthily jumped down from the window to the parapet. While jumping out on the parapet, she heard the security siren go off. Immediately the bungalow got lighted up by flash lights and a guard reached below to catch her.

She jumped, slid down the pole and hit the guard with full force. The guard lost control and fell on the ground. Around the same time, the other guard was kneeling over from another window. He jumped on the parapet and slid down over the pole to catch her. She jumped and covered the gap between the bungalow and the trees within a few moments. While running she heard a shot behind her which was fired by the second guard by his .303 rifle. The bullet had hit the wall. She escaped and jumped behind the bushes.

She then jumped over the boundary wall, ran up to her car which was parked around the bend, and sped away.

KJ was agitated and held the security guards responsible for the break in. He gave them a dressing down for their lack of alertness. He deliberately did not inform the police, because he knew it could lead to unnecessary trouble for him.

KJ realized that there were two ways to retaliate. The first one involved taking bodily revenge by enemy action. However, he found himself limiting in this approach.

The second one was through professionalism. That approach required him to reestablish himself as the king of Bollywood. It looked like an impossible task after suffering the financial losses. He was fretting due to the deterioration in his condition. He realized that from being a producer of hit films, he was reduced to being a caricature. His self image had taken a beating. He realized that Bollywood had found younger players who were full of energy and new ideas.

He decided to take revenge through his devious plans for the last and final time.

15

Ranbir held *The Times of India*. The news on the cover page at the lower section had Meera's photograph and an article on her.

"Meera, well-known heroine of the film world, gets the prestigious Padma Shri award for her charitable work. Her trust fund has created scholarships for meritorious poor students so that they can carry out the professional studies in the field of Information Technology in the three cities of Pune, Bangalore and Hyderabad."

Ranbir felt very happy and proud of Meera that she had acted so nobly to contribute to the society. He picked up his mobile and called her up to congratulate her.

"Hello!"

"Hello Ranbir, it is nice to hear your voice."

"I wanted to congratulate you. You are doing a remarkable job."

"Thanks for your wishes. I'd like to ask you something. Will you be my guest during the award ceremony in Delhi?"

"Oh sure, it will be my honour!"

The award ceremony was two days later at Vigyan Bhawan.

Meera and Ranbir arrived together but as she was one of the awardees, she was seated in the second row along with the other awardees. Ranbir took a seat in the third row along with other guests. The President along with the Minister of Culture arrived in a few minutes. The President and the Minister were handed bouquets of flowers by the master of ceremony and then were escorted to the podium. The President gave a small speech to honour the awardees.

Meera was invited on stage and the President handed her the medallion. The function went on magnificently.

After the award ceremony Meera and Ranbir walked to the courtyard for the luncheon. The courtyard was elegantly decorated.

There were beautifully laid out carts with traditional vegetarian and non vegetarian food and fresh fruit juices.

"This is a facet of your personality I did not have an inkling of," Ranbir said.

"I was a female star in the glamour world. I knew that my professional lifespan was short. So I looked for an alternative career and I chose to be a social worker."

"You are a wonderful person. You should think about your own personal life as well now."

"I have been unlucky in my personal life. I had two disastrous relationships, first with Karan and then with KJ."

"Maybe in both your relationships, you gave more importance to wealth rather than the persons you were getting hitched to. You can let that pass and move on."

"Yes, that was the mistake."

Meera overtly acknowledged Ranbir's point of view. However, in her heart, she compared her and Ranbir's positions from a different perspective.

She was thinking about the inequalities in the social system. She realized that by the time Ranbir was settled, she had failed in two personal relationships. At the same time he also had three relationships – with herself, Sunanda and Veena. Both of them had their share of fame and fortune, however in the male dominated society, she had been conditioned to think of being at a disadvantage. On the contrary, even after having three affairs, he was considered macho and virile. She pensively arrived at the conclusion that in the male-dominated world, men and women didn't compete on a playing ground of the same level.

Ironically, at a subconscious level, she had overlooked two major differences between them. The first was that Ranbir had relationships with herself, Sunanda and Veena. All of them were open-hearted and good women. Whereas Meera had jumped into relationships with Karan and KJ, both selfish people who lacked in humane qualities.

The second difference was that Meera was a heroine in the glamour world, where the lifespan for the heroine was short. On the other hand, Ranbir was a producer and a director; the role where quality improved with experience.

It was almost eleven by the time they reached back to the hotel lobby.

Finally they shook hands and Meera said, "Ranbir, I am so happy that you joined me for the function. Please keep in touch."

"Meera, the pleasure is mine. It is a great honour for you. I wish you all the success in life."

They bade each other good night and proceeded to their suites.

16

KJ had known a few underworld gangsters during his twenty-four years of experience in the film world. He had recruited Badshah from the same underworld contacts more than two years back. Badshah was loosely connected with Chhota Rajan's gang. He was a middleman in their drug dealings. He also acted independently with Chhota Rajan's approval as he shared a part of his earnings with him. Chhota Rajan had allowed the arrangement because he knew that Badshah had the particular penchant to blackmail the rich and famous.

KJ had sent a message through one of his contacts for a direct meeting with Chhota Rajan. The meeting was confirmed at Hotel Victoria near Opera House after three days. It was a shady hotel and KJ knew that it was risky to meet there, but he didn't have any choice. So he went there with an assistant who carried a large suitcase and two armed bodyguards.

Chhota Rajan was already waiting on a swivel chair in the centre of a large semi-dark room. His deputy, Manya and an armed bodyguard stood behind him while two muscled men stood near the entrance, one on each side. Manya as well as all the bodyguards held revolvers in case of any threat to their boss. Chhota Rajan was a lean, dark-complexioned man in mid forties. He had a tattoo of a tiger on his right lower arm. Even indoors he wore dark goggles. KJ stood opposite Chhota Rajan. His bodyguards also held revolvers in their hands, ready to shoot. KJ's assistant stood on his left side with the handle of the suitcase in his right hand.

KJ was perspiring but he mustered strength and wished Chhota Rajan in a flat tone, "Hello, how is the business?"

Chhota Rajan came to the point without wasting any time on civilities, "Tell me, what do you want?"

KJ initially lisped yet he came to the point, "I want Ranbir and Veena dead."

Chhota Rajan didn't go into the details of his motives and his response was professional. "What makes you think that I will accept the contract?"

"I can give you some vital information against them, which will give you enough reason to take action even without my contract."

"Tell me!" Chhota Rajan looked at him with curiosity.

"One of your gangsters, Badshah was murdered by them."

"Are you sure?"

"Yes, they murdered him and disposed his body by putting it into his own Innova and hurling it over a hill at Nalasopara."

"Why couldn't police nab the culprits?"

"The police had concluded that it was a case of drunken driving, because they had recovered only parts of his charred body and car. The police did not have the inclination to pursue the case as he was a drug dealer and a blackmailer."

"Then how was he killed?"

"I knew that he was blackmailing Ranbir and Veena. They took revenge and murdered him."

KJ showed him a photograph of Badshah and Ranbir exchanging an envelope with a briefcase near Hotel Taj Lands End at Band Strand.

"How is Veena involved? Besides being a known heroine, she is a minister's daughter."

"Ranbir had succumbed to Badshah's blackmail twice over an interval of ten months. Ranbir had paid him large sums in exchange of some of his scandalous photographs with Sunanda because he could not fight back. Only when Veena, who was the new heroine of Ranbir's last film *Noora* was blackmailed was Badshah murdered. She is vindictive!"

Chhota Rajan looked hassled as he let the information sink in.

"OK, what is your offer?"

"Four crores! I am paying two crores as advance and the remaining two crores will be paid after they have been bumped off!"

KJ signaled his assistant to pass on the large suitcase containing the currency notes.

"Okay, it is a deal!" Chhota Rajan said and signaled Manya to take the suitcase.

KJ wished Chhota Rajan and they dispersed without wasting any time.

17

Chhota Rajan had accepted the suitcase containing two crores. While his Toyota Fortuner was passing Dharavi, he thought that he needed to clear some doubts. He asked Manya to call up Inspector Jatin.

Manya dialled Jatin's number and once he heard his voice, he handed the mobile to his boss.

"I know you had investigated Badshah's case, how come the police report concluded that he had died due to drunken driving and his Innova had skidded and fallen off a cliff at Nalasopara?" Chhota Rajan asked.

"Salaam Bhai! That is what really happened!" Inspector Jatin responded in a matter of fact tone. He was nervous in speaking to the Mafia boss.

"I have got information that he was murdered by Ranbir and Veena because he had been blackmailing them."

"He did blackmail Ranbir twice and each time he paid him twenty lakhs over a gap of ten months. He did not murder him because he is not a violent man," Jatin replied without showing his nervousness.

"What about Veena?"

"Veena was not involved; she was not blackmailed."

"I may be wrong or your investigations may be incorrect. I will not spare you in case you have lied to me." Chhota Rajan threatened.

"It was an open and shut case, Bhai. The police department did not spend too much time on it." Jatin was confident by then.

"Fine then!" Chhota Rajan was about to switch off the phone.

"Bhai, how come you remembered Badshah all of a sudden, fifteen months after his murder?"

"It just came to my mind!"

Chhota Rajan responded without revealing any more details and disconnected the phone. He had become alert. He thought hard.

It struck him that Badshah, his henchman had been cheating him. He had received a hefty forty lakhs from Ranbir but he had given him just four lakhs. Badshah worked under his tutelage and was supposed to pass on a major share of the money to him. Chhota Rajan angrily thought that Badshah deserved to be killed.

Chhota Rajan analyzed KJ's motives as well. He realized that KJ and Ranbir started their careers as film producers in the same way, with a gap of fourteen years. When KJ's career was at its peak, Ranbir was an upstart. But in the last eight years, Ranbir had become a well-known producer and got international fame, whereas KJ's career had nosedived.

KJ had been jealous of Ranbir's success, therefore he planned to tarnish his image. He employed Badshah directly without his approval to take Ranbir's scandalous photographs. However Badshah upstaged him and directly blackmailed Ranbir. Badshah later tried blackmailing Veena. Chhota Rajan also concluded that Badshah met his end in the accident while he was driving under the effect of liquor.

KJ married Meera, who was once Ranbir's love as well as the female lead in his films to spite him. But he could not undermine Ranbir as he had moved on and he was romantically involved with Veena. He also failed to cause any dent in Ranbir's success story. To KJ's utter disappointment, when his own film flopped at the box office, Ranbir's film broke box office records.

Finally KJ didn't have any more options left and he approached him.

Chhota Rajan was not inclined to bump off a well-known producer and a known heroine, and that too the daughter of the Minister of Tourism at the Centre. He figured out that the contract killing amount was too less in comparison to the risks involved. To top it all, he was convinced that KJ was a thug because he had bypassed him, when he had employed Badshah without his permission. He finally decided to call off the deal.

Chhota Rajan called up KJ through his deputy's mobile.

"Hello, I have second thoughts. I am not interested in your supari. My man will deliver your suitcase in an hour."

"Why, you said it was a deal!" KJ was shocked.

"I never back out, but in this case, I do not want to be involved."

"I can increase the amount if that is the reason."

"I don't want to discuss this matter further."

Chhota Rajan disconnected the line thereafter. KJ was shocked and felt helpless as he steered his BMW towards his bungalow.

Within the next forty-five minutes, a man came and returned his money.

18

Inspector Jatin sat in his Scorpio and sped down the Expressway. Fifteen months had passed since he had investigated Badshah's case. In his report he had concluded that Badshah had died due to negligent driving under the effect of liquor. Inspector Jatin had carefully omitted the part about Badshah being a blackmailer. He himself had been suitably rewarded by Ranbir and Veena for protecting their reputations by deleting their names from his report. He thought that Badshah could have had four enemies – Chhota Rajan, KJ, Ranbir and Veena. Badshah didn't have any public sympathy; therefore the news about his death was not worth a dime.

Chhota Rajan as well as KJ had remained quiet these fifteen months. Inspector Jatin was surprised to receive a call directly from the Mafia boss asking him about the cause of Badshah's death. He concluded that after Badshah's death, KJ might have tried to target Ranbir and Veena on his own. When he could not cause them any harm, he would have contacted Chhota Rajan and offered him the contract. That is when Chhota Rajan learnt that Badshah, his gang member did not die due to negligent driving, but he was murdered by Ranbir and Veena.

Inspector Jatin immediately rang up Ranbir.

"This is strictly confidential information! I do not want to disturb your peace of mind, yet being your wellwisher I want to warn you. I have learnt through reliable sources that you and Veena are the targets of an underworld contract killing operation. Most likely KJ could be the conspirator and Chhota Rajan's gang could be the executor."

"Thanks for the information. We will be cautious."

Ranbir immediately met Veena and informed her about inspector Jatin's warning.

She smiled snidely as she recalled KJ's pitiful face from her last meeting. She realized that KJ was still trying desperate measures.

"I know KJ is planning to finish us, let me handle this!" She reacted confidently.

Ranbir advised her, "Don't risk your life by directly meddling with KJ. He has been nursing his wounds for a long time. His contracting Chhota Rajan's gang to murder us…means that he can go to any lengths to harm you and me."

Veena looked defiant but she didn't discuss her plans.

Ranbir decided to get security guards for both of them.

Chapter - VII

1

KJ got up with a start; he saw Veena in her mask towering over him. She was attired in her black rubber outfit and was holding her Wesson pistol against his head.

He was perspiring profusely in spite of the air conditioning. He saw that the door and all the windows were closed. He marveled that how she had managed to sneak into his bedroom despite all his security arrangements.

She allowed him to calm down. She removed her mask and sat down on a chair on the opposite side with her Wesson pistol still pointed at him. She was silent and relaxed.

He looked dumbstruck.

"Why, I have not done anything!" KJ said defensively.

She got up and slapped his face.

"You are a scum, you don't deserve to live!" saying that she straightened the pistol close to his head.

He looked worn and defeated. He lowered his head to beg her for mercy.

"I think you have forgotten my last warning. You contracted the underworld to finish us off?" she asked in a cold, threatening tone.

He was shocked that his plans to murder her and Ranbir had leaked out and his action plan had boomeranged.

"I am sorry I made a mistake." He confessed in a low tone.

"Do you think we will just let you carry out your dirty plans?"

He begged her to grant mercy. As the last resort, he bent down and prostrated in front of her.

She spitefully looked at him and then she locked her pistol and put it in her pocket.

"OK, I am sparing your life for the last time; you mend your ways and do not cross our path." She warned him, took a few steps back and opened the window. She peeped out and stealthily jumped out of the window to the parapet and slid down the pole. She made a few quick strides and jumped out of the boundary wall.

KJ was not sure that whether she had really left. He lay petrified and after a gap of five minutes when there was no movement around, he nervously walked up to the window and looked out. He called his guards, realizing that she had escaped.

After that daring show, Veena forgot about KJ, because she was convinced that he had become inconsequential in their lives. She knew that in spite of his evil designs he could not cause any harm to them. She was sure that her threats had pacified him.

2

ZEE TV had organized the Annual Film Award show in an auditorium at Santacruz West. They had announced that the profits of the show would go towards the welfare of the family members of the Mumbai police. Meera's trust *'Ujagar'* had announced one full residential scholarship for IT studies in each of the three city universities in Hyderabad, Bangalore and Pune for the meritorious students from the families of the Mumbai Police.

Ranbir, Veena, and Meera were present as a part of the film fraternity. Inspector Jatin was also present as part of Mumbai Police.

The function started with a cameo role by Veena in her debut film *Noora*. She looked very pretty and her short portrayal impressed the audience in the hall and lakhs who were watching the program live.

After some performances, the awards were announced. Ranbir was awarded the best director award and Veena the best actress for *Noora*.

Meera was invited as a VIP to present the scholarships to the three students. Among the students who won the scholarships were two girls and one boy.

Mumbai Police Commissioner, who was the chief guest of the show, expressed his special appreciation for the film industry for organizing the charity show for the welfare of the families of police force and also for Meera's trust for giving scholarships to the youngsters from Mumbai police families.

KJ was conspicuously absent at the function.

While the function was going on, KJ watched the show on television, with a glass of whiskey in his hand. He had slipped from a position of strength in the same glamour world to being a recluse. He lived in the west block of his bungalow, while his family lived in the eastern part. On that evening, his pain became unbearable, and he became extremely dejected. He poured his third stiff drink to help him endure the loneliness. A few years back he had everything going for him. He was applauded for his achievements and he had a big following. At that time he was at the peak of success and the same people who were being awarded were either unknown or mere beginners. He regretted that he could have retired with prestige and he could have been a respected figure among the film fraternity but he chose the wrong path. He had been arrogant and had started manipulating situations in his favour. He realized that instead of physically chasing other people's jobs, lifestyles and women, he should have chased his own imagination.

He was rejected by the aam aadmi who had made his films hits in the past. His own film fraternity had rejected him. He was so dejected that he decided that he would not suffer any more. He opened his cupboard and took out a small bottle containing sleeping pills.

He scribbled on a note pad, "I am committing suicide due to my unhappiness. No one else is responsible for my death." He dropped a number of pills in a glass of water and swallowed them. He lay on the bed and switched off the lights.

Next morning, KJ's servant found his body when he brought tea for him. The servant raised the alarm and KJ's son, wife and daughters came rushing. They were shocked to find him dead. They found his suicide not and also recovered the bottle of sleeping pills.

They called the police and within fifteen minutes, an inspector with three constables arrived. The inspector checked KJ's corpse and entered an FIR in a notebook. Within half an hour, the media also arrived.

The film fraternity was shocked that one of their senior members had had such a tragic end. The TV news channels reported that KJ had committed suicide by taking an overdose of sleeping pills. He was reported to be under severe depression after his last three films flopped.

3

Ranbir and Veena were very much in love with each other. Ranbir had been very successful professionally as well as in his personal life. He wanted to settle down with the girl who had given him all her love. Ranbir proposed marriage to Veena which she happily accepted. She was also wholeheartedly in love with him and regarded marriage to be the culmination of their love.

Sudhakar Naik announced the forthcoming marriage of his daughter, Veena with Ranbir, the famous director.

Ranbir sent invitations to his brother and his family in Bathinda.

The marriage function was lavishly organized at JW Marriot Hotel at Juhu. Many bigwigs had been invited.

The decorated lawn resounded with shehnai from Ustad Bismillah Khan. The area was beautified with gladiolas, roses, lilies and marigold flowers. The green henna hedges were illuminated with coloured lights. The decorated sofas, tables and cushioned chairs were arrayed around the big lawn. The guests arrived in groups and were welcomed by Sudhakar Naik and Veena's other relatives and friends. In a short span, part of the lawn got filled up with guests. The guests were served drinks, starters and sweets while they waited for the arrival of the baraat. The whole atmosphere was lively and colourful.

Veena was dressed in a red sari with a golden border. Her beautician had delicately applied mehendi on her hands and feet. She had her hair curled; she wore a gold necklace, red and green glass bangles on her forearms.

Soon the baraat arrived. Ranbir as the groom was dressed in a white sherwani, golden kurta and pyjama. He was riding on a white mare. His head was partially covered with a sehra made with strings of night blooming jasmine. He was escorted by his elder brother, sister-in-law, nephew and niece. His office staff and friends from the film community were present. When the baraat arrived at the entrance, the contingent of baraatis danced on the beats of the dhol.

There was a short ceremony that included the introduction of the bride's relatives to the bridegroom's relatives. The latter were offered gift packets by the bride's relatives as the onlookers showered rose petals.

The ritual was followed by cocktails and a sumptuous dinner for all the guests, family members and the staff.

Two of Ranbir's ex-loves Meera and Sunanda were conspicuously absent, though they had been invited. Ranbir missed them but he respected their wishes. In his heart, he always wished well for both of them.

The marriage was solemnized with Ranbir and Veena taking seven rounds of the fire and taking vows to be together for the rest of their lives.

4

Ranbir and Veena sat on the beach at Versova. It was late at night, the sky was clear and a light breeze was blowing. The waves were shimmering under the moonlight. Ranbir had put his arm around Veena's shoulder.

"I love you darling." Ranbir said.

"I love you too," Veena said.

Ranbir felt a little playful and he needled her, half in jest and half in seriousness.

"Why do you love me? I am only an ordinary man; you are a minister's daughter."

"Your tongue and cheek comment is not welcome. My dad's position is temporary, whereas as you have already made a name as a well-known director!"

"Still…I don't see myself worthy of you!"

"A gem doesn't know its value. Only a connoisseur can assess it correctly."

"We will change the subject." While saying that, he bent over her and kissed her on the lips.

"Whatever happens, we will always be together," Veena said.

"Let's go to Venice for a holiday. The two of us sitting on a gondola is my picture of romance," Ranbir said.

She heard him and the words meant so much to her. She was like a little girl amazed by each syllable that he uttered. She felt that probably it was what true love felt like; it was the culmination of her dreams. She felt elated and she looked beyond the stars into the distance. She held his head and brought his face close to hers and gently kissed him on the forehead.

Ranbir realized that before meeting her, he had become a cynic and he had stopped believing in the existence of true love.

"You have been my protector. I have been very lucky to get your love," he said.

Veena got overwhelmed by his compliment. She remembered the efforts which she had put in to get him the contract for the three documentaries, arranging the finance for his film, silencing Badshah, and getting rid of the police trail as well as KJ's threats.

He embraced her and kissed her on the lips. He promised to love her all his life. She meant more to him than all his fame and wealth.

"Look beyond the horizon. I shall love you till eternity." He promised.

"I also love you from the bottom of my heart," she responded.

"We will have a small cottage in a beautiful place and we will call it our nest!" He said.

She nodded in agreement.

Their conversation carried on till they reached back home and fell asleep in each other's arms.

5

KJ Junior was uncontrollable when he saw his dad's corpse on the bed. His name was Rajkumar, but since the time he had come to Mumbai after completing his graduation from Yavatmal in Maharashtra, he was called KJ Junior.

The police had reported the cause of death to be suicide. His mother, sisters and the film community believed that KJ had taken his own life due to the financial setbacks. KJ Junior looked at his father's bedroom, critically visualizing the scenario of the previous evening and the circumstances which had led his Dad to take his own life. He discovered that the last program recorded on the TV was the Annual Film Award show.

He switched on the program and called the two guards in the bedroom. They watched the clips together. They looked at Veena's show in her cameo role.

Rajkumar pointed towards Veena on TV and asked his guards, "Was she the intruder who had sneaked in his Dad's room at midnight?"

The guards were very surprised to hear his question. They were serious and they stressed their memories. The first guard confirmed that the intruder was a woman in tight fitting rubber clothes but he could not confirm whether she was Veena, who had sneaked in as her face was masked. The second guard supported KJ Junior's version, and confirmed that the intruder was similar in height and physique to Veena.

Rajkumar was convinced that his dad had been humiliated by Veena. He bitterly reflected about the sequence of events. He concluded that she was responsible in making his Dad's life miserable.

He swore loudly, "I will not spare her. I won't let her go scot free."

Rajkumar had just stepped into his Dad's shoes and he had no record of crime. He expressed his deep anger against Veena to his two buddies, Sid and Peter. They promised to extend their full support to him. They decided to devise a fool-proof plan to finish her.

Rajkumar was unforgiving; a characteristic he had inherited from his Dad. He had discovered his Dad's private diary in his safe. He had found some underworld names with phone numbers there. One of them was Manya with CR written in bracket. He knew that his Dad had used his underworld contacts in his days.

Rajkumar called up Manya from his Dad's mobile.

He heard the mobile ring and after three rings, the call got disconnected. He knew that Manya was aware about the caller's identity.

In a few seconds, he got the call from a landline on his Dad's mobile.

He picked up the mobile and said, "Manya, I want to offer Chhota Rajan a contract to finish off someone."

"Who are you? Why are you calling from KJ's mobile?" The caller questioned.

"I am KJ Junior and I want to have a meeting with Chhota Rajan and you."

"Why do you think we will take up the contract?"

Rajkumar was tongue tied; he did not have convincing reason. Even then he uttered, "I can offer a sum which he can't refuse!"

There was a pause. Rajkumar knew that Manya was in consultation with his boss and they were contemplating about the bait. He was tense while he was holding the mobile to his ear. After a lapse of two minutes, he heard Manya's voice again, "Come to Hotel Victoria, Room 101 at Opera House."

6

Veena was arranging her wardrobe when she received a message:

"I will take my revenge. – KJ Junior."

She was shocked to get the message in her inbox of the e-mail account on her iPhone.

She looked at the sender's email account address.

She noted that the email was sent from KJ's company address, email@ kjmovies.com. She felt squeamish because it was an open challenge by KJ's son and the inheritor of KJ Production.

She had never met KJ Junior and she didn't even know his real name or his age, but obviously he held her responsible for his dad's suicide. It was ironical that when she felt secure in her cocoon of power, money, fame and love that she was being threatened by a novice. She realized that she could not take the threat lightly. Obviously KJ junior had done some research before pinning the responsibility of his dad's death on her.

She looked into the address and phone numbers of KJ Production and called KJ Junior. He himself picked up the phone and spoke, "Veena, you had driven my Dad to commit suicide. I swear I shall not leave you in peace!"

Veena responded with full élan, "KJ had left a suicide note in which he had taken full responsibility of taking his own life. I don't know what you are talking about. You better stop threatening me! Do you know who you are talking to?"

"I know you are some minister's daughter! I will not allow you to move freely after committing the heinous crime." KJ junior challenged her.

"Okay, I did what I did. Let me see what you are capable of," Veena responded angrily.

"You will not live long to show your arrogance!" KJ junior affirmed.

She disconnected the line.

Initially Veena was upset and thought of seriously discussing the threat with Ranbir. She remained uneasy for sometime, but later on, she brushed aside the whole episode as an emotional outburst of a spoilt brat. She misconstrued that the whole episode did not merit any move from her side.

7

Rajkumar kept two crores in a suitcase and summoned his two buddies, Sid and Peter. He warned them about the risk and only after they promised their support, he left with them, armed with revolvers and the suitcase containing the cash.

They were cautious as they were going to have a meeting with the underworld don in his own territory.

They reached Hotel Victoria and were whisked to a large semi dark room where Chhota Rajan sat on a revolving armchair in the centre.

Rajkumar wheeled the suitcase to the room, with Sid and Peter following him. They were ready to draw out their revolvers in defense in case of any attack from the underworld gangsters.

Rajkumar stood at a gap of three metres from Chhota Rajan and his deputy.

Chhota Rajan did not waste any time and got down to business.

"Your dad offered a contract price of four crores to murder Veena and Ranbir a few days before he committed suicide. I had refused his offer. I understand that you have come with a better offer. Tell me, I am all ears!"

"My offer is four crores to murder only Veena," Rajkumar replied.

Chhota Rajan contemplated and looked towards Manya; they both looked acquiescent.

"Okay, that is acceptable. How are you making the payment?

"I am paying you two crores now and I shall pay you two crores after the job has been done," Rajkumar replied.

"It is a deal!" Chhota Rajan confirmed and signaled Manya to take the suitcase.

Two days later, when Veena was driving to Oberoi Trident for a press conference, her car was intercepted by three cars. Three armed men got out of the cars and fired at her. She was severely injured. She was in intense pain and bleeding. She picked up her mobile and pressed Ranbir's number.

While she lay gasping for breath, she heard the familiar harsh voice, "You had made the mistake of threatening my dad!"

She opened her eyes in severe pain and she saw KJ Junior disguised as a bearded middle-aged man. He looked resolute, towering above her. And then there was the final shot. She died instantly.

8

Ranbir was devastated to learn about Veena's murder. He had earlier talked to her about security, but she loved her freedom and was fearless.

He immediately drove to the spot where she had been shot. The police had cordoned the area. He was allowed to go to the car. He saw her empty car riddled with bullets. There were blood stains all over. The armed murderers had escaped in three cars before the police could arrive. The police had wired messages on all the posts in south Mumbai with the details which they had obtained on the basis of the reports on the scene of crime.

Ranbir was informed that Veena's body was taken for post-mortem to Bombay Hospital. When Ranbir reached the hospital, he was guided to the mortuary. He was totally shattered when he saw her bullet-ridden body. In a few minutes, Veena's dad also arrived. He was also in a state of shock. Both were numb. After their visit, the body was sent for post-mortem.

The police had commenced a high level investigation to catch hold of the murderers. A hunt was on to trace the three cars. The police was also interviewing the eye witnesses. According to their account, there were three masked armed men who had come in three cars. They had fired with their revolvers. A fourth man had walked through to see the victim. One more round was fired by one of them. All the three gangsters escaped in the three cars. The fourth man also fled.

The film community as well as the public mourned Veena's violent death.

The police could not nab the murderers even after two days. They concluded that it was a gruesome operation most likely executed by the underworld because the cars used in the operation had been stolen. The cars were found abandoned at different locations. They had also concluded that the murder was obviously a vendetta executed through contract killing.

On the fourth day of Veena's death, to pay homage, a shanti sabha was organized at the Tata Auditorium, at Nariman Point.

Veena's smiling portrait was placed on a table in front of the stage.

The condolence meeting was addressed by a master of Paramhansa Yoganand.

"Veena lived a happy and cheerful life. She was a loving daughter, an investigative journalist, an accomplished actor, and a devoted wife. She had many qualities such as courage, liveliness and a unique charisma. She has left an unforgettable impression on all those who came in contact with her. She in a way touched and enriched their lives. We should remember what Ben Jonson had said in his poem. 'It is not growing like a tree in bulk…. A lily of a day is fairer far…'

We pray for her soul to rest in peace." The discourse was followed by a few group devotional songs.

In the end the attendees walked to Ranbir and Sudhakar Naik to share their grief and to pay homage to the departed soul.

9

Inspector Jatin had become quite close to Ranbir over the past few years.

They met once again to discuss the identity of Veena's murderers.

Inspector Jatin looked resolute while he shared his views with Ranbir, "Veena most likely threatened KJ, who felt so defeated that he took his own life. KJ Junior could have been emotionally hurt by the tragedy. There is no proof about him being responsible for Veena's murder, but there is a fair possibility. He was most likely the fourth person who was at the spot, when Veena was murdered. He was in the make-up of a middle-aged bearded man and later disappeared in the crowd. I am trying my best to find evidence against him."

Ranbir nodded in agreement and they parted.

Inspector Jatin spent the next two months following KJ Junior's activities. He tried to find out whom he interacted with, and how he spent his time. Jatin finally derived that KJ Junior was keeping himself clear from the underworld to avoid any suspicion on him. He seemed busy with re-establishing his Dad's floundering business.

Jatin conveyed his findings; he added that he would intensify his efforts to nab the criminals. Ranbir thanked him for his efforts.

Ranbir had been deeply saddened by Veena's death, but he had to let go of the past and decided to move ahead. He was non-violent by nature. He believed in the Hindu philosophy of karma, therefore he knew that he didn't have to bother about KJ Junior's mental state or his emotions of vendetta. He elevated his thought process. The tragedy of Veena's death had made him think deeply about the very purpose of his own life.

It dawned on him that he could provide immense service to the society. He had been privileged to be able to communicate with lakhs of people through the medium of his films.

Sudhakar was unaware of Veena's circumstances and therefore couldn't understand what anyone could have had against her. With a lot of agony, he had to accept his daughter's violent end. He also repented the futility of his pursuit for power and his own greed for money. He took retirement from politics and decided to spend the rest of his life in social service. He went to his birth place at Baramati and donated a major portion of his wealth to set up a multi-specialty hospital, where poor could get medical facilities free of cost.

Sudhakar also emotionally supported Ranbir and allowed him the freedom to choose his own path.

9

Sid and Peter had moved to Versova to a two room apartment after Veena's murder. They did not have any role to play in the execution, but they were privy to the underworld operation and the huge amount of money which had changed hands.

They were jobless but because their buddy Rajkumar had inherited a film production unit, he compensated them with financial rewards. They spent all their time in loitering around.

Once Sid was driving with Peter near Juhu beach.

"What will we do once we exhaust our cash?" Sid asked.

"I never think about tomorrow!" Peter replied.

"What do you say about that one? Sid shifted to the lower gear and drove the car to the right side of the road. He whistled and lustily stared at a young girl in her twenties jogging on the road side in a tight top, shorts and skids.

The girl shouted, "You bastards!"

Sid stopped the car and reversed it and drove it near her.

"Oh come on hot pants, we can have fun together!"He told her unashamedly.

By now Peter too was staring the girl.

He shouted, "Babe we will take good care of you, hop into our car!"

As no one had come to help her, the girl bolted from the spot.

Sid and Peter drove away and carried out their girl hunting activities all day.

At night they visited Kamathipura, a red light area. While they were inside Studio 22, a brothel waiting for the call girls, they heard a sudden commotion. One of the prostitutes warned them that the police had raided the place. They hurriedly put on their clothes and escaped from the back exit.

The experience jolted them. Their money was fast depleting and they thought about meeting Rajkumar. It finally happened in an unexpected way when they landed in a serious situation, which compelled them to visit Rajkumar.

"We have no place to go, the police have tracked us," Sid and Peter uttered to Rajkumar nervously.

Rajkumar was tense; his buddies' untimely visit had given him a big jolt.

"Tell me what happened?"

"We thought that the deal called for a celebration. We walked towards Metro Bar. Three girls were performing a pole dance and about twenty customers were watching the show. We took seats opposite each other. We ordered scotch with soda, a packet of Marlboro cigarettes and a plate of chicken spring roles.

"Two sexy busty bar girls in low cut blouses and maxis joined us. They introduced themselves as Lily and Jennifer. They asked us if we could buy drinks for them. We were more than happy.

"We found the girls attractive and put our arms around them. They were cooperative and they drew closer. In a couple of minutes they invited us to two ante rooms where we had sex. We wanted to pay the girls but they refused. We were a bit intrigued and we mistakenly assumed that the girls were attracted towards us.

"Thereafter, we had paid a few more visits to the bar. During one of the visits, inadvertently we blurted out the episode about the murder.

"In our subsequent meeting, a man joined us. He introduced himself as Inspector Jatin from CID. The girls had recorded our conversation with them in which we had bragged about the murder and they had sold the tape to Inspector Jatin. He knew everything about you and your dealings with the underworld to murder Veena. He wanted our confession which we unwittingly had already given.

"The present predicament is that if we become police witnesses in the court then we might get a pardon or we might get a lighter sentence. Unfortunately, you will either get a long term or you will be sent to the gallows."

Rajkumar looked ashen after hearing his buddies.

Sid and Peter left after that. Rajkumar was holding his head, tormented by the situation. He was gripped by fear when he received the dreaded call.

"Hello, am I speaking to KJ Junior?"

"Yes."

"I am CID Inspector Jatin. I have solid evidence against you about Veena's murder. I have submitted my report along with the evidence to police commissioner. I want you to come to the CID head office near Victoria Terminus in two hours."

Rajkumar had felt absolutely numb; his plan had misfired. The whole matter had unfolded in the most unexpected way. His buddies whom he thought were his confidants had betrayed him.

He contacted his lawyer, Mahesh.

"Deny everything and ask for your right to communicate through your lawyer only. They can't do anything until you are proven guilty," Mahesh guided him.

He made his next call to Manya, "The cat is out of the bag, and unwittingly my two buddies have confessed that we had executed Veena."

Manya first sounded irritated but later he cautioned him, "Don't worry! They will turn hostile in the court, you don't admit anything; neither to the police, nor in the court."

Rajkumar felt lighter after that.

He deleted the call records from his mobile and left for the police HO.

The police filed the case in court and the trial on theVeena murder case proceeded on the due date.

The police had charged Rajkumar alias KJ Junior as the main accused. The court ordered him to stand for trial. The prosecution lawyer levelled the charges of conspiracy and cold-blooded murder against him. Sid and Peter were the co-accused, whom the prosecution presented as police witnesses.

Mahesh as the defence lawyer argued that the police was unable to catch the mafia gang, who as per the FIR had executed the murder in broad daylight on a busy highway in Mumbai.

Inspector Jatin was shocked to hear the two witnesses. When interrogated by the defence lawyer, they retracted their statements. They said that their recorded statements were false because at that time they had merely bragged to their girlfriends under the effect of liquor. Jatin understood that the witnesses had succumbed under pressure.

Jatin was distraught and unhappy as his witnesses had turned hostile. He angrily drove out of the court and headed to meet Ranbir.

Ranbir's wounds were reopened when Jatin narrated the entire episode. Veena's sweet memories crowded his mind once more. He imagined the whole chain of events, including the final cowardly act of the spoilt brat, KJ Junior. He was unable to come to terms with the fact that the police of the metropolitan city of Mumbai had been unable to deal with the underworld thugs.

He lamented before Jatin, "Why are we living? Is it in any way better than the law of the jungle? I can't bear the loss of my wife. She was a remarkable woman. She has been murdered by the underworld at the behest of a maniac. Shockingly, the law and order agencies have been unable to apprehend them."

Jatin heard him and consoled him by holding his hands.

He sympathized with him, "I am sorry for your loss, I will try whatever I can to bring the criminals to justice. The next hearing is after two days."

10

Inspector Jatin had just received the tip from a reliable source that Chhota Rajan gang was receiving regular supplies of heroin from Afghan smugglers. The next motor boat with supplies was due to arrive at Daman beach at 10.00 pm. It was 1.00 pm and he had limited time to act. He got permission from the Mumbai Police Commissioner to strike and got his team ready.

The police raid was successful. Jatin was overwhelmed that Chhota Rajan himself was arrested in the operation.

In the court, on the day of hearing, Chhota Rajan was produced by the prosecution as the head of Veena's contract killing operation.

Chhota Rajan confessed to his crime and gave his testimony against Rajkumar alias KJ Junior. He admitted having received four crores to murder Veena. He also confirmed that three of his gangsters – who were in custody – had stolen three cars, had stopped and attacked Veena. The final shot was fired by KJ Junior himself.

Judge gave the verdict, "Rajkumar alias KJ Junior had contracted Chhota Rajan to murder Veena to take revenge. The murder was executed by a gang of three and KJ Junior. KJ Junior will serve life term for murdering Veena. Chhota Rajan and his three hit men will also serve life sentences. Over and above, Chhota Rajan and his three hit men will be tried on other charges separately. Sid and Peter will serve one year jail term each for being accessories to murder and giving false testimony in the court."

11

Ranbir continued to be unhappy and morose for days, but being a creative person, he finally took charge of his life. In the past he had been able to get over his sorrow by immersing himself in work. He applied the same principle and tried to get over Veena's loss by keeping busy with work.

Ranbir's new film got completed three months later. He was at the Hyatt Regency in Delhi a few days later and was pleasantly surprised to see Meera standing next to him. She had come to have dinner at the China Kitchen with a group of friends. She looked as beautiful as always.

"Oh what a pleasant surprise, how come you are here?" Meera enquired smilingly.

"It is a wonderful coincidence! I have just returned from LA and I am in Delhi for three days for some meetings in the Turner International office. How about you?" Ranbir replied.

"I am so glad to see you here. I have a meeting with the Ministry of Education regarding certain grants for my trust. I am staying nearby with Taruna, my IP college friend. In case you are free, then tomorrow we can spend some time together!" Meera said.

Ranbir readily agreed. They chose to meet at the lobby at eight the next morning.

Ranbir was meeting Meera after a gap of two years. He had become more mature and spiritual during this time. He laid greater importance to the inner qualities of a person. He did not know so much about the changes in Meera but he could make out that she had become a socially responsible person and her trust was helping the less fortunate. She looked dignified and giving.

They went for boating to Badhkhal Lake. They had enjoyed an outing there fifteen years back when both had been freshers in Delhi University. They were reliving the memories of the past.

"Meera, you had told me that you wanted to become a film star fifteen years back at this very place, and that's how I decided I wanted to get into film production." He remembered with nostalgia.

"We were so full of dreams!" Meera reminisced.

"I understand that we have passed through many experiences… good as well as bad during the period, but I think we have been destined to be one," he expressed his love.

She kept quiet and looked at the waves. She realized that he was unhappy and lonely.

"Meera, it is fortuitous. I had always been in love with you." He persisted.

She saw Ranbir looking at her with complete sincerity. She herself had been in and out of love a few times. She thought deeply as she couldn't afford to make a mistake this time. Finally the meaning of his words sank in her head. She realized that after all, she was also in love with him. She was lucky that fate had given her the final chance to be one with him.

She changed her seat, came into his arms and both kissed each other. It was the moment of sheer ecstasy.

She saw a pair of swans, and she pointed towards them with a smile.

They experienced the same love for each other as they had during their first boat ride together. They locked in an embrace and kissed once more.

Ranbir proposed to her, "Will you marry me?"

Meera replied, "Yes, I will!"

Meera and Ranbir had seized the opportunity. This was how it was always meant to be.